Jalen & Colby

A DADDY FOR CHRISTMAS NOVEL

HJ WELCH

Jalen & Colby
A Daddy For Christmas

Copyright © 2023 by HJ Welch

Cover Design by Jo Clement

This book is a work of fiction. Names, places, and incidents are either products of the author's imagination or are used fictitiously. Any resemblance to actual events, locales, or persons, living or dead, is entirely coincidental.

Jacked Up (D/s – Jack and the Beanstalk)

Trigger Warning

This book features mention of past homophobic abuse from family members, including religious conversion therapy. There is also a nonviolent on-page homophobic confrontation.

CHAPTER 1

Andreas

I THINK I MIGHT HAVE ACCIDENTALLY STARTED WORLD War III.

Taking a break from the impassioned bidding currently happening on my computer screen, I sigh, rubbing my chin and feeling the stubble that's more like a short beard after several days of not shaving. Usually, I like to keep my appearance smooth and sharp. But after many days of rummaging through dusty boxes, I can't say I care much right now.

Looking out over the edge of my balcony, I slowly inhale the warm evening air. Even though I've been down under for a few years now, it's difficult for me to think of December as being the height of summer. It's hard to argue with this gorgeous weather, though.

I close my eyes and allow gratitude to wash through me. Immersing myself in this frustrating task might have left me feeling grumpy at this particular moment, but I do know I live a very charmed life.

The ding of another bid comes through on my eBay listing, making me wince. I glance from the laptop through the sliding patio door at the dozens of items I currently have laid out in my living room. The door is closed to keep the cool air in, but the lights are on, and now that night is coming down, I can see everything illuminated well.

When I moved my whole life from London to Sydney, I didn't have the time to deal with sorting my stuff out. I just had most of it shipped halfway around the world and packed away into a storage unit where I didn't give it all a second thought.

Until now.

I had an embarrassing amount of holiday left to use before the year ran out, so I figured it was finally time to open everything back up and take a look. When I uprooted my life five years previously, I literally packed everything. All the crap I'd been shuffling from place to place since I graduated uni almost twenty years ago. I didn't even know what half of it was anymore. I just kept it out of habit.

And what a lot of rubbish there was sitting there waiting for me when I unearthed it all again this week.

It's crazy how much I've just chucked into the bin. Some nostalgic bits and bobs are now proudly on display in my Mosman apartment, which overlooks the bay, giving it a little more character than the lifeless state it's been in. It's still pretty soulless, I'm sad to admit, but it's a start.

What was left in the faded cardboard boxes, I'm now selling.

It's not like I need the money in the slightest. It's more that I can recognize that these items might not spark joy for me anymore, but I can see they would easily be valuable or cherished by others, and I like the idea of giving them second lives in new homes.

Except 'joy' isn't exactly what's sparking right now online.

I wince as the bids keep going up and up. I'll admit, when I sorted everything out to photograph so I could sell it on eBay, some stupid kid's toy wasn't what I thought was going to be the most hotly contended item. I've thrown an Omega watch on there for a quarter of its original price, for crying out loud. But nope. The thing that's going nuclear is a battered, very much preloved set of space dinosaurs and the action heroes who ride them.

Jurassic Galaxy was one of those bonkers nineties TV shows that was almost certainly cooked up by studio execs after they'd snorted a bit too much of the good stuff. Even though I was slightly too old for it when it came out, I became mildly obsessed with the brightly colored dinos and their zany human companions. It probably had something to do with the fact that the lead guy was actually *Black*. That wasn't something I saw much of at all when I was growing up.

It's funny that I really didn't want to get rid of the set of action figures. I've displayed them in every place I've lived since I collected them in my teens. But when I looked around my fancy Sydney pad, it didn't feel like they fit anymore. Getting rid of them seemed like the right thing to do.

Secretly, I'd hoped they wouldn't get any bids. Then I could justify boxing them back up and putting them under my bed or something. But whoever these two people are… they mean business.

The listing is ending in less than ten minutes, and they've suddenly gone on a rampage, trying to outbid each other. That's pretty standard in online auctions, as far as I know. People will often try and swoop in at the last second to snatch the prize from under everyone else's noses.

But this is getting a little ridiculous between JayBird-Queen94 and Sunshine_Dino. I initially put the collection of toys up for a measly ten Australian dollars, but they've currently bumped themselves up to over eighty and aren't showing any signs of stopping.

These action figures really aren't worth that. They are

properly scratched up, their joints are loose, and the poor triceratops is missing the end of his tail. Years ago, I fancied maybe trying to restore them by freshening up their paint and perhaps making that poor fellow a new tail with molding clay or something. But I talked myself out of it as it seemed frivolous and not the sort of thing a man of my age should be doing.

I think that's why the bidding is getting to me. I'm regretting ever listing the set for so little, like it never meant anything to me. Whoever these two bidders are, they're showing me just how valuable the toys actually are, despite what I might have tried telling myself.

It's too late to back out now. I wince as I watch the seconds tick down to zero, and it really is a matter of luck who gets the final bid in. At a whopping ninety-five dollars, the winner is Sunshine_Dino, and I can't help but let out a sigh of relief that it's over. Sadness washes over me as I look over at my beloved collection. My only solace that whoever the new owner is, it seems that they'll care as much or even more about these little guys than I have. As I do.

I puff out my cheeks again and shake my head, deciding that a glass of wine is in order. I head back inside the coolness of my flat and into the kitchen to pour one, reminding myself that this is for the best.

For a while now, I've been thinking that I need to try seriously dating. It's been ages since I brought a guy home, and when I do, I want to give the right impression. Now that I'm in my late thirties I'm starting to understand what kind of boyfriend I'd like to be. It helps being older, I think, because I know that I really enjoy taking care of younger, sweet guys. Not that there's been one of those in a good while, with how busy work has been. But if I set my heart on finding someone, I want to assure them when I bring them home that I'm up to the task of taking care of them.

Battered kids' toys do not scream reliability, even if they're hidden in a box somewhere. *I* need to know that I'm mature and responsible. So this is all for the best.

It takes at least half the glass before I can pretend to myself that's true.

With a rueful chuckle of resignation, I finally make my way back out to the sectional sofa I have out on the large, covered balcony, and take a look at my laptop. I was expecting the notification that I'd made a sale, but I'm surprised to see two messages waiting for me to read.

One each from Sunshine_Dino and JayBirdQueen94.

I frown as I settle down with my wine and figure I'll read the message from the winning bidder first.

Sunshine_Dino: Hey, andylad2000. I just won the Jurassic Galaxy action figure set you put up on eBay. Thank you for that, BTW! Merch for JG is so rare, but it's my favorite TV show. Actually, it's my best friend's fave show too, that's why I was so determined to win it. I know it'll be the perfect Christmas pressie for him. But, um, I got a bit carried away and didn't realize *how much* I was bidding—oops. Is there any way I could pay you in installments? I know this set is going to mean the world to him, but I'm not sure I can afford it all right now. I'm so sorry. If you want to relist it, I understand. Thank you for your time.

My heart melts. What a sweet message from someone who's obviously a great friend. I want to tell him to screw the money. I don't care, but I'm not sure how eBay would feel about that. Before I make any decisions, however, I decide to check out the rival bidder's message as well.

JayBirdQueen94: Hey andylad2000!!!!!!! OMG that bidding was INTENSE. LMFAO cringe. So I totally understnad that I wasn't lucky this time but I was really hoping u might hav some more Jurassic Galaxy stuff??? That show is the WHOLE REASON me & my BFF even met & I know hed just DIE for a Xmas gift like that. I saw form teh listing that ur based in Sydney—US TOO!!! Well Mount Druitt lol. Id totally be okay comming & meeting u in person if it meant I could gaurantee getting something for my bestie?? PLZ PLZ let me know. Its r first Christmas IRL & I want it to be PERFECT! Hugsssss

JayBirdQueen94 closes their message with several kissy face emojis. In fact, their whole message is littered with crying faces, praying hands, and sparkling hearts, not to mention an eye-watering number of typos. Their enthusiasm is adorable.

My mind is whirling. I frown as I flick back through the pages and check the address where I'm supposed to mail the action figure set to.

Mount Druitt.

Rather than jumping to conclusions right away, I pick up my empty glass and wander back inside for a refill, mulling over the information that's been given to me. When I come back outside, night has properly fallen, but I've got the over-head recessed downlights dimmed low, so it gives me a cozy glow as I carefully read through both messages again.

No, I'm sure. These two users are each other's best friends, both trying to buy the same gift to surprise each other this Christmas.

If I thought my heart was aching before, it's nothing compared to now.

After a nice long sip of wine, I place my glass down and start thinking this through. I never wanted any money for my beloved toys. If I was going to let them go, I just wanted them to find a new home where they'd be treasured.

There's nothing to say they couldn't be loved by *two* different people.

An idea is already forming hard and fast. I promise myself not to make any decisions until the morning when I'm sober and have had a chance to sleep on it. I do *not* want to come across as creepy. Fuck no. But Christmas is a time for going the extra mile in the name of joy, as far as I'm concerned.

Either way, whatever happens next, I decide that I've got some work to do before these little guys go anywhere. I pull out a frozen dinner to shove into the oven, pour another glass of wine, then get busy.

'Tis the season, after all.

CHAPTER 2

Jalen

It's been a couple of days, and I still haven't heard anything from andylad2000 about any other Jurassic Galaxy stuff he might have. I know it was a long shot to even ask, so I shouldn't be disappointed. But I'd be lying if I said I wasn't totally bummed about missing out on the greatest gift I could have gotten for my greatest friend.

Of course I am coping well with the devastation.

"Um, Jay?" a sweet voice says from what I assume to be the threshold of the living room. "Are you okay?"

I lift up the sparkly mask that's currently covering my eyes and kick my long, skinny legs, which are hanging over the arm of the chair where I'm draped sideways. My starlet gauzy robe with the ostrich feather trim fans out like a butterfly, and I sigh dramatically before taking a sip of the mimosa I poured myself the moment the clock struck five.

"I'm perfectly fine," I squeak at him, fluttering my false eyelashes. "Why do you ask?"

Colby snorts and hugs himself as he ventures into our sparse front room. Everything in here we've scraped together from thrift stores—or op shops as they call them here in Australia—because we're broke AF, and all our money goes on rent. So I can't *really* be mad that I didn't get into an ADHD hyperfocus frenzy and spend stupid money on a frivolous Christmas present. But when I look at how adorable Colby is as he perches on the edge of the armchair with me, I know it would have been worth every cent.

"You're moping," Colby accuses gently.

It's my turn to snort. "I'm…adjusting to a disappointing situation," I clarify with a pout. I've been tempted to confide in him about the perfectest present I almost managed to get him, but I eventually figured it would be too sad for both of us. It's better that I keep hunting for something else from Jurassic Galaxy and tell him the story afterward when it can be funny.

The thing is, that silly TV show saved Colby's life, and I know it. We were both a bit too young to watch it when it came out in the nineties. But unlike a lot of shows from that decade, it still holds up really well, so a ton of people like us discovered it in our twenties when it got uploaded to streaming.

The reason it's so beloved is due to its diverse cast, I'm sure. I saw myself not only in the characters with different skin tones but the queer-coded ones as well. They even had a girl who alternated between using her wheelchair and riding a pterodactyl. It feels like it was written by people other than straight white dudes—in fact, I know it was. It might have only gotten three seasons, but I think that's a good thing. It meant they didn't get a chance to ruin it.

Colby and I met on a chat forum dedicated to all things Jurassic Galaxy. His home life was so hard with homophobic, overly religious parents who tried to control his every move. This TV show and the power of the internet offered him a desperately needed escape. More than that, it gave him the chance to make real friends, even if they lived on the other side of the world.

I was just a nerd who absorbed facts like sunlight and indulged in all kinds of whacky conspiracy theories. But Colby wrote the most incredible fanfiction that I would devour from my bedroom in my parents' house in California. I was his fan before I was his friend, and couldn't believe it when I found out he was younger than me.

I wish he still wrote fics. He's so dang talented. But he works so much it doesn't leave a lot of time or energy for creativity. Things will get better someday, though. When they do, I'll be right here in person to bully—*ahem*—gently encourage him to stretch out his fingers again. It's so much easier to support him now that we're in the same time zone, let alone living together.

He smiles at me, and I brush my fingers through his sandy blond hair, my heart giving a little flutter. I still can't quite believe that we only met in real life for the first time this summer. Or winter, as far as Colby was concerned. Whatever—July. Videocalls don't count.

As far as *I'm* concerned, my life began again the moment I ran through the arrivals gate at Sydney Airport, screaming as I launched myself into my waiting best friend's arms. I love him *so so* much, and getting that super rare action figure set would have shown him just how much I care about him.

Because it wasn't some set you could buy in a store, no ma'am. It was a collection that someone had obviously put together themselves from individual toys. Not someone. andylad2000. *Urgh.* I try not to be angry at them for letting someone else win the bid and then not bothering to respond to my message, but…well, I'm a petty bitch. If it were just for me, I wouldn't have cared so much. But it's for my baby *Colby.* He deserves the world after everything his horrible family put him through.

I shake myself and smile for my baby. "How's your day going?" I say, changing the subject. "How was work?"

I'm fully aware that Colby has no interest in the store where he kills himself taking as many shifts as possible to make his half of the rent. Well…what he *thinks* is his half of the rent. I might have been a bit sneaky and told him it was less so I could contribute more to ease his burden, even if it's only a little. My crappy office job might mostly involve mind-numbing data entry and too many coffee runs, but it pays a few hundred a month better than Colby's paycheck.

I'm here on a working holiday visa, so I know I'll only have to put up with temping there for another six months at the most. After that…I'm not sure. I can't apply for another visa like that because I'll be thirty, and that's the upper age limit. I don't know what I'll do because now that I've found Colby, I can't possibly leave him.

But that's a worry for another day. Right now, I've still got to find the perfect Christmas present for my bestie. Or second most perfect, I guess. Nothing is ever beating that action figure set.

Colby shrugs in response to my question about his job and runs his fingers over some of my purple feathers. I bite my lip and repress a shiver, reminding myself for the MILLIONTH TIME that my more carnal feelings for my best friend need to stay locked up tight in that box I've buried deep in the depths of my soul.

The thing is…I had an inkling that I was probably in love with Colby a few years ago. But it was always so safe when I was back in California and he was just words on a screen. Things got worse after we started video calling and I finally knew how his voice tinkled like a bell and his smile fluttered like a butterfly when it wasn't frozen in a photograph. Meeting in person just compounded every single fantasy I'd ever had about us by a hundred.

And then we moved in together. Because I'm that much of a dumbass.

I know with MY WHOLE HEART, though, that my baby needs someone the complete opposite of me to date. It's simply a fact. I'm a walking disaster, and he needs someone responsible. And when that day comes and he meets this hypothetical man, I will let him go with grace.

Because I have to.

"I've been looking for seasonal work," Colby says, breaking my train of thought. He's not meeting my gaze, but I blink anyway.

"On top of the job you already have?" I ask. How many hours does he think he has in the day? The boy needs to sleep.

He shrugs again. "I need the money for Christmas."

I frown and shake my head. "Hey, no," I say. I don't want to rub things in about his family, but I don't want him making himself sick, either. "You only have me to get something for, and I already told you I'd literally die of happiness for a candy bar. Boo-boo! All that matters is that we're here. We're going to go to the beach on Christmas Day like we said and get drunk on cheap wine. We don't need anything else."

He blushes and looks away from me. My heart skips a beat, but I tell it NO! Behave.

"I might have *already* bought you a present," he mumbles.

My damn heart skips again. "Baby, you shouldn't have," I say softly. How much money has he spent?

He chews on his thumbnail. "I thought I might be able to pay for it in installments, but the whole amount came out of my account already, and I'm not sure what to do."

"Col-bee," I say, stretching his name out into two syllables like I always do when I'm trying to make him listen properly to me. "You shouldn't have splashed out like that, but I'm very touched you did. Don't worry about getting any extra work, though. I'll get the groceries this week."

He bites his lip and looks at me with his beautiful blue eyes. "I'm sorry I spent all that money. But—Jay. Seriously. I think you're going to *love* what I got you. I couldn't believe it when I found it!"

My heart expands, and I link my hand with it, bringing it up to kiss the back of his fingers. "You're so cute," I murmur. His cheeks flush again and my pulse quickens. It's in moments like this I can imagine leaning over and kissing much more than just his fingers. *Urgh!* I love him so much! I wish…

I'm saved from doing something monumentally stupid by the doorbell ringing. Like I'm coming out of a trance, I laugh, kiss his fingers again with a loud "MWAH!" then jump up to answer the door.

We live around the back on the second floor of a dreary brown apartment building. We rarely get cold callers, and it's too late for the mailman. It might be an Amazon delivery or something, but I know I haven't ordered anything, and I doubt Colby has with how he's worrying about money. Ohhhh, maybe they're Christmas presents from my family? My mom said she was sending gifts for both of us because she knows Colby's douchebag homophobic parents have cut him out of their lives.

Their loss. He's amazing and they deserve to walk on Legos forevermore.

With a dramatic swoosh of my floor-length purple gauzy robe (because what's the point of having it if I don't make the most of it?), I throw open the door with a big smile, popping a hand on my hip.

Then I freeze.

It doesn't look like a mailman, but *phew,* he sure is delivering *something.*

"Hi?" I utter, blinking rapidly and wondering how fast that mimosa has gone to my head. I'm pretty sure I didn't order a hunky Daddy, but here one is anyway.

The guy has dark skin and beautiful eyes that sparkle with mirth. He's about my height but, like, twice as stocky. Even through his jeans and T-shirt I can see his sculpted, lickable muscles. I'd guess he's in his mid-to-late thirties, so about a decade older than me.

A perfect Daddy age.

Yeah, sue me, lol. I'm so lovesick over my best friend that lusting after a stranger is, quite frankly, a welcome distraction. Colby isn't so sure, but I'm convinced we both need handsome Daddies to look after us. I was into that scene when I briefly lived in LA. In my fantasies, our Daddies are also best friends so that Colby and I can still see each other all the time as well.

"Hi," the guy says with a sheepish smile that I swear to god could stop traffic. "I hope this isn't weird, me turning up like this unannounced, but I'm looking for Sunshine_Dino or JayBirdQueen94."

"You're British," I say, playing with the feathers on my collar. If I had long hair, you can bet I'd be twirling it. "Wow, that's so cool. Oh! Yeah, I'm JayBirdQueen94. I don't know who…" I blink. Actually, I *do* know who the other person is. "Sunshine_Dino? That's the jerk who outbid me on eBay! Wait?" My brain is working extremely slowly. I blame the half a mimosa I drank. But I finally register the box Mr. Handsome is holding in his hands. "Are you andylad2000?"

He chuckles as Colby appears at my elbow. He's shorter than me, even when I'm not wearing fluffy heeled slippers, so he comes up to my shoulder. "Did you say Sunshine_Dino?"

"Yes, I did," the guy says, looking relieved. He turns his gaze back to me. "And yes, I'm andylad2000."

I blink and look at my best friend. "How did you know

that…? No!" I shriek and bat his arm. "Is that you? How did I not know your eBay handle?"

Colby frowns at me. "What are you talking about?"

I drop my head back and laugh, feeling weirdly relieved. "Christina on a cracker, does that mean you won the Jurassic Galaxy set that I was trying to buy for you?"

His eyes go impossibly wide. *"You're* JayBirdQueen94?" he cries. Then he blinks and probably thinks about the name some more. "Of course you are. Oh my god."

I wave my hands with a flourish. "The one and only." I look at andylad2000 again. "Did you know?"

"I worked it out from your messages, yes." He looks at us both with such warmth it makes my skin tingle. "I wanted to deliver the collection in person and surprise you, seeing as it's a Christmas present for the both of you."

Tears pool in my eyes as Colby and I share an incredulous look. "I can't believe we were trying to buy it for each other," he whispers faintly.

I grab his shoulders. "And now we can SHARE it! Eeekkk! This is amazing!" I start dancing on the spot before remembering that we have a guest. "That's so sweet you came out to deliver it in person! Would you like to come in?"

"I'd love to," he says, and we make room for him to step inside. "I'm Andreas, by the way."

"I'm Jalen, and this is Colby," I tell him, hugging my bestie to my side as Andreas closes the door behind him. "This is like a Christmas miracle! Come in, come in. Would you like a drink? We have lemonade or iced tea, or a beer if you like?"

"Iced tea would be lovely," Andreas says as we make our way back into the living room. I shove Colby into the armchair that I was previously lounging on and shoo Andreas onto the sofa. I don't mind playing host and getting us drinks, and then I can sit on the beanbag.

"Did you take the train?" I ask as I bustle into the kitchen, grabbing glasses.

"Uh, no, I drove," Andreas calls after me. "I'm out in Mosman, so it only took about forty minutes."

Mosman? Jesus, this guy must be rich. For a second, embarrassment flashes through me at him being in our shabby little apartment out in Mount Druitt. But then I remember what my mama always said. "Good manners are the greatest wealth of all, mijo. It costs nothing to be kind and polite."

In no time at all, I sweep back into the living room with an iced tea for Andreas and a mimosa for Colby. If he's half as shocked as I am, he's going to need it.

He's got the box Andreas was carrying in his lap. As I sit down, he looks between me and our guest. "Shall I...?"

"Gaga on a go-kart, *yes, girl!* Open that pretty baby!" I blink and turn to Andreas. "Oh, if that's okay with you?"

He laughs. It's a beautiful, low, rumbling sound that makes me shiver. "Of course. Why don't you boys open it together?"

I giggle and wiggle my fingers. "I guess we could?"

Colby looks at me with such affection. "Yeah, let's open it together, Jay."

I know he just sees me as a friend—and that's ABSO-LUTELY for the best. But damn it, if doesn't make my heart stutter.

I gleefully crawl over to him and attack one end while he tears into the other. My false nails aren't very useful in this situation, but before I can ping one off, Andreas is by my side, offering me his pen knife.

"What a Boy Scout," I purr, flicking my eyes over him and making him laugh. I might seem confident and flirty on the outside, but in reality, I'm glad I'm already kneeing down because he's turned my legs to jelly. Seriously, where did this British hottie come from?

In seconds, Colby and I have the box open, and my jaw drops when I see that Andreas has carefully packaged the action figures in beautiful sparkly black tissue paper.

"It looks like space," Colby says softly, running his fingers over the tissue.

Andreas grins. "That's what I thought," he says warmly.

Whelp. He makes me feel like I've won a gold star, even when he's not talking to me. I can see by the way Colby blushes that he likes it as well. Who the hell is this guy? Where did he come from? The North Pole directly from Santa?

Carefully, we begin fishing through the tissue paper and pulling out the toys. My heart is pounding in my chest with each one we uncover. But then I get to Jesse, the triceratops, and I pause, looking him over carefully.

"I thought his tail was broken?" I say uncertainly. The eBay listing Andreas made was totally upfront about the fact that these figures were very much preowned and well loved. I didn't mind that they were battered, but as I look at all those we've revealed so far, I swear they look shinier.

Andreas clears his throat and rubs the back of his neck. "I decided to do a few repairs and touch-ups. I hope that's okay?"

I blink at him and look back at the orange dinosaur in my hand. "It's perfect. He looks brand new! You did an amazing job."

"I'm a graphic designer," Andreas admits. "I enjoy arts and crafts. It was my pleasure to fix him and the rest of them up for you guys."

He holds my gaze until I feel my pulse quickening again. I laugh and look away, shaking my head incredulously. "This is amazing. *You're* amazing."

"Seriously, thank you," Colby says.

He's cradling Buckets to his chest. That's his favorite character, the guy the fandom pretty much unanimously agrees is dating his sassy robot best friend. As Spark is voiced by a male actor, that makes it a queer relationship, which is pretty awesome considering when the show was made. Obviously, nothing happens to confirm this in the canon, but Colby's written enough fanfics about those two to more than make up for it.

Soon enough, we have all the figurines out of the box standing proudly on our coffee table. I feel a little emotional. I was so sad when I lost the bidding war, but it worked out even better this way. I love the idea of sharing the collection with my best friend in the whole world. We never would have connected if it hadn't been for these characters in front of us.

"Oh," I say to Colby, a thought suddenly occurring to me. "I should pay you half of what you spent on eBay. It's a present for both of us, after all."

Before Colby can reply, Andreas is shaking his head and reaching into the back pocket of his jeans. "I forgot. Colby, this is for you."

He hands over an envelope. Colby takes it and looks inside, his eyebrows rising. "Is that…?"

"A hundred dollars," Andreas confirms with a nod. "You paid ninety-five dollars plus a couple of quid for postage, so I rounded up."

"But…?" Colby says with a frown. Andreas is already waving his hands, though.

"I don't want a penny for them," he insists. "I just wanted them to go to a good home. Seeing the way you guys fought to give them to each other showed me that's exactly where they'll be."

Colby bites his lip and glances at me. "That seems greedy,"

he says quietly.

Awww, my baby. He's so damned sweet, always thinking of others. He never thinks he deserves nice things, because his awful family made him believe that for so long. I move over so I can wrap my arm around him.

"No one could *ever* accuse you of being greedy, sweetie," I tell him.

"Honestly, it's my pleasure," Andreas says sincerely.

Colby looks between me, him, and the toys on the table. "Okay," he says softly. "But only because it's Christmas."

That makes us all laugh.

The moment stretches out. Andreas is looking thoughtfully at us both snuggled on the armchair. "I, uh, guess I should go," he says, but he doesn't sound convinced.

I don't blame him. We've barely known him for fifteen minutes, but the thought of him disappearing already makes me panicky.

"No!" I yell, then blush in embarrassment. "I mean…if you already have plans, of course you should go. It is Friday night, after all."

"I don't need to be anywhere," he says, his eyes sparkling as they meet mine. "In fact, I'm off work until the new year. I've been catching up on life admin." He gestures to the table, and I wonder if he's put more things on eBay that he doesn't want anymore.

"You could stay for dinner?" Colby suggests.

I laugh. "We don't have much food here, but you'd be more than welcome."

Andreas bites his lip, his eyes flicking between us. "I could take you boys out to dinner?"

My heart almost stops entirely in my chest. Mr. Handsome wants to *take us out to dinner?* What kind of Christmas daydream is happening right now? "Uh, yeah!" I cry, turning to nod feverishly at Colby. "We'd like that, right? That sounds super fun!"

"That's very generous of you to offer," Colby says slowly, and I can already tell he's worrying about money.

So can Andreas, apparently. "Not to sound like a dick," he says with a gorgeous lop-sided grin, "but I'm offering to pay for all of us, so don't worry about that. It's not every day I meet fellow Jurassic Galaxy fans. We need more time so I can hear all about your favorite episodes."

"No Big Deal," Colby and I cry immediately in unison. It's the episode where the heroes' spaceship breaks down, and we see flashbacks of all the characters as they fight to survive. It's the best because it's when the asshat character, Ricto, finally becomes one of the team instead of their enemy.

Andreas lifts his eyebrows in appreciation. "Good answer," he says with a nod.

"What's yours?" Colby asks breathlessly.

Andreas winks at us. "I'll tell you over dinner. How about that?"

I glance at Colby, checking he's okay with this. He's not great with surprises or changes to his routine. But he's all rosy-cheeked and starry-eyed as he gives me a little nod in agreement.

"WOOHOO!" I shriek, making Andreas jump and laugh as I launch myself onto my feet. I pull Colby up after me. "Let's get our glad rags on, baby doll. We're going *out* out!"

CHAPTER 3

Andreas

What am I doing?

Part of me feels like this is a really, really bad idea. I just met these sweet guys. It's got to be absolutely nuts that I've whisked them into the city for a fancy meal. But I can't argue with myself because it feels completely right and natural.

When they finished getting out all of the Jurassic Galaxy collection, I couldn't bear the thought of leaving so soon. The invitation to dinner just blurted out of my mouth. And it's weird because it kind of feels like a date, but there're two of them, so genuinely, I have no idea what's going on.

But I know I'm having fun.

Jalen, the American, is a total firecracker. His outfit for dinner consists of heeled boots, wide-legged trousers with a tapered waist, and a sparkly vest top. He's wearing bright eye shadow, shimmery lip gloss, and bangles on his wrists that clack with every elaborate hand gesture.

Colby is like a shy little puppy, but he looks at everything with such wonder it's beautiful. He's not got Jalen's flamboyance, but they both have an honest, earnest vibe to them, just on opposite ends of the spectrum.

"Thank you so much for everything," Colby says again as the waitress takes away our menus. Having made a quick internet search and found absolutely nothing decent near the boys' place, I decided to bring us back to Sydney to a Thai place near me that I know and love. I've ordered Champagne for all of us, so I'll just pop the boys in a taxi to take them back home.

I don't want to think about them leaving just yet, though, so I push that thought aside.

"I reckon that's about the thirteenth time you've thanked me," I tease Colby gently with a wink. He blushes, and my heart flips. Jalen takes his hand and kisses the back of his fingers.

"Andreas is right," he says with a laugh. "It's cute, though."

I wonder yet again if they're a couple. They've mentioned several times that they're best friends, and that was how they described one another in their initial messages to me. But they're so casually affectionate, and I've caught them both looking at the other with longing in their eyes. I can't help but feel like there's a story lurking under the surface.

"When I put those toys up for sale, I didn't expect any interest in them," I admit. "Let alone that I'd get to meet a couple of fellow fans. You both must have been pretty young when it came out, though?"

I'm fully aware that I'm fishing for their ages to make sure nothing about this is weird. But they are definitely a good few years younger than me, so I don't think it's a bad thing to find out.

"Yeah, I'm twenty-five, and Jalen is twenty-nine," Colby says with shining eyes. "We caught it on the second wave, when it was released on streaming."

"We became, like, totally obsessed," Jalen adds with a dramatic hand laid on his heart. "Queer brown characters running around space on dinosaurs? Hell to the yeah! Waaayyy better than real life."

He's said a couple of things like that. "Was life hard for you back then?" I find myself asking before I realize how personal such a question is, and completely inappropriate considering we only met a few hours ago. "I'm sorry, that's none of my business."

Jalen shrugs. "I was okay, I guess. But who doesn't need a little escapism from life, right?"

It's a good way to sidestep my blunder, so I smile and nod, then ask them about their work instead. Jalen starts regaling us with anecdotes about his office job that he clearly doesn't care about. But I notice that Colby has gone quiet, simply watching his best friend with a sad, wistful look in his eyes.

It pulls on all my heartstrings. I'm drawn to both of these young men, but there's something about Colby that reminds me of a wounded bird. I just want to wrap him up warm and take care of him until he can fly on his own again.

"So what's *your* job," Jalen asks with a flick of his eyebrows before taking a sip of his Champagne. We've finished our appetizers and are currently waiting for our mains to be brought out. "I bet it's way more interesting than working in an office or a shop."

I want to argue that there's nothing wrong at all with either of those jobs. But it's clear that they both hate what they do for work and are still struggling to make ends meet with what they earn. So I don't insult them by trying to convince them that their lot isn't so bad. Plenty of people in their twenties have stepping-stone jobs. I really hope that these two young men get the chance to pursue their dreams soon enough.

"Well, like I mentioned before, I'm a graphic designer," I say, looking between the boys.

It makes my heart skip a beat to see them giving me their rapt attention. To them, I probably seem older and wiser, when in reality, I feel like at thirty-seven, I'm still fumbling through life just as much as I was doing ten years ago.

"Is that what brought you to Sydney?" Colby asks. It makes me so happy whenever he's brave and speaks up. I don't miss that Jalen beams at him proudly for asking the simple question.

"Yep," I tell them, pausing a minute as our food arrives.

After I thank the waitress, I continue with the story. I kind of want to skip over it and save myself some embarrassment, but at the same time, I also want to ensure that when I tell these boys that dinner is on me, I really, truly mean it.

"I was lucky, though. My first job over fifteen years ago was as an intern at a large company back in London. They got the opportunity to design the logo for a social media group that was just starting out. Snippet."

As usual, when I tell this to people, it only takes a second for realization to dawn on their faces. "Snippet?" Jalen repeats.

"The video app?" Colby splutters.

I nod and take a second to sip some creamy tom yum soup from my spoon, not wanting to let it get cold. "They had their top designers working on the pitch, but one of them was my mentor, and when I showed her something I'd worked on, she threw it into the pile for consideration without telling anyone who'd come up with it."

"She wanted to claim your work as her own?" Jalen says with a frown, sitting up straight. I try and repress a grin at how adorable he is for getting defensive on my behalf a decade and a half after the fact.

"No," I say with a shake of my head. "She didn't want them to dismiss me because I was only an intern. She told them right away once the client selected my work as their favorite."

Colby's jaw drops open, a forkful of pad Thai hovering in front of his mouth. *"You* designed the Snippet logo?"

"I think I was in the right place and the right time more than anything," I start to deflect, but Jalen isn't having any of it.

"Katy on a kite! That's so cool! So…did you get a commission or whatever, or did your company take credit?"

Again, I shake my head. "Obviously, it did the company a lot of good, and they got paid handsomely, but yes, I got an individual bonus as well as earning royalties from the company so long as they use my design."

Jalen looks at the Champagne and back to me. "So you really are rich, aren't you?"

"Jay!" Colby yelps in horror, smacking his friend on the arm. Jalen just laughs, though.

"What, baby cakes? You were the one who was worried about Andreas spending money on us. I'm merely pointing out that he probably has a lot of it to spare."

I chuckle at his bluntness. He's not wrong. I tilt my head and give Colby a reassuring wink. "I do have a few quid knocking about. It's nice to be able to spoil some new friends. Especially at Christmas—it's the time of giving!"

Colby finally puts his fork down and bites his lip for a second. "That's really nice of you, Andreas. Thank you." He leans over and hisses into Jalen's ear with a scowl. "That doesn't mean we can be greedy, though."

I can't help but laugh and so does Jalen, but Colby doesn't look hurt. In fact, his expression is mollified. "I pinky promise to behave myself," Jalen says, holding up his little finger.

Colby rolls his eyes and links his own finger with him. "Let's not go that far," he mumbles, making me laugh again.

"But if Andreas can really afford all this easily…well, I'm just going to say thank you for the fifteenth time."

I grin as I reach over and squeeze his arm in a reassuring manner. "You're very welcome, hun. And anyway, like I said, it's all purely selfish. I just need some friends in real life to geek out with over Jurassic Galaxy."

Jalen's eyes go wide. "We haven't even heard what your favorite episode is yet!"

Colby shakes his head. "I really want to know, but do you mind if I use the men's room first?"

"Of course not," I say sincerely. "I promise not to discuss anything interesting until you return."

"I'll be quick!" he says earnestly. He jumps from his seat and hurries through the restaurant, nearly knocking into a waiter in his haste.

"So you're a sugar Daddy."

Jalen's words stun me so much I almost pull a muscle with how fast I snap my head back around. I stare at him with wide, slightly horrified eyes. "No! Of course not! That's…I'm not…"

He laughs and shakes his head as he pats my hand. "It's not an insult. Sorry. You give off such Daddy vibes that I thought you were in the scene."

I blink as I collect my thoughts, aware that I probably don't have much time before Colby comes back, and there's probably a reason that Jalen brought this up the second he left the table.

"I don't…I mean, I've never…" Wow, this is going well. "It's not a bad thing?"

Jalen is unusually calm and sincere as he squeezes my hand. "It's a kind of kink where someone gets pleasure out of spoiling another person or lots of people. It's not necessarily sexual or anything. The other person gets their kicks out of being treated super special. Like they're not used to believing they matter, so they need extra reassurance."

Why do I get the feeling he's not talking about himself right now?

"Oh," I say, thinking over his words. "I guess…yeah. That's exactly what I'm doing here, isn't it?"

Jalen nods, the sparkle back in his eyes. "Just so we're clear, I'm having a *marvelous* time, and so will Colby once he chills out. I assume you're not expecting anything in return. Although you are gay, aren't you?"

I splutter again. "No! I mean…sorry, yes. I'm gay. But of course I don't expect *anything* in return!" I swallow and make an effort to lower my voice. No one's looking our way. However, I'm only a decibel or two away from creating a scene. "That's not what this is about at all."

Jalen bites his lip and looks like he's trying to stop himself from laughing. "Oh, you poor baby. I *know* that. That's what I'm saying, Sugar Daddy. I just thought I'd clarify so we're all on the same page. And by 'we', I mean you and I, because Colby will need a little looking after either way."

"By you?" I ask.

He shrugs. "By both of us, maybe. You want to treat us, right?"

I toy with the stem of my Champagne flute. "Is that weird? We only just met."

Jalen shakes his head. "Not at all. In fact, it fits right in with the whole sugar Daddy thing. We can be your sugar babies for an evening, and everyone has a good time, yeah?"

His eyes light up, and I don't have to look over my shoulder to see that Colby's coming back. Knowing what I do already about him, I suspect that something in his past has made it tough for him to accept kindness, gifts, or any kind of affection, probably.

That only makes me want to try and take care of him harder.

But…it's not just him. I glance at Jalen as Colby sits back down, watching the easy way this sassy boy leans in to bump shoulders with his best friend. He's already launching into another funny story about the last time he tried to use chopsticks and how he accidentally catapulted a prawn into the hair of the lady on the next table over. "You know, chopsticks aren't actually a Thai thing, but most restaurants offer them now anyway," he tells us.

I marvel at these two young men and consider the ton of information that Jalen just dropped so unexpectedly into my lap.

Honestly, I definitely thought being a sugar Daddy was a seedy thing. But the way Jalen described it is exactly how I've been feeling for a while about what I want in a relationship. I don't want to be a power couple and date someone else with millions in the bank. I want to nurture and take care of somebody. I want to help and guide them. I want to spoil them.

Just like how I want to spoil these boys.

Jalen said that it didn't have to be a sexual relationship. So…what if I take this surprising new relationship with these two boys and use it as a sort of…practice? I could test out how to be a sugar Daddy and see if it's what I'm really craving. There's no chance Colby would allow it to become something grubby, that I can already tell. In fact, I don't think Jalen would, either, despite being utterly fabulous and flamboyant.

It's obvious from their flat that these guys barely have two pennies to rub together. What harm could there be in me in spoiling them a little? Maybe more than a little.

It is Christmas, after all.

CHAPTER 4

Colby

"Go on, then," Jalen asks as the waiter comes with a third bottle of Champagne. "You never told us *your* favorite episode, Andreas."

I'm feeling all giggly and tipsy. It's helping me to stop worrying so much about, well, everything. Why Andreas is spending all this money on us. Why he took the time and effort to hand-deliver the Jurassic Galaxy set to us in person so we could share it. Why he fixed up the more broken figures just to give them away to us. Why he wants to hang out with us now.

It's not in my nature to accept good things. In my experience, everything comes with strings attached. Yet Jalen's just rolling with it as if rich guys take us out to dinner all the time.

It's not just the money, though. Andreas keeps looking at us as if we're the most delightful, interesting, adorable things he's seen in a long time. Or maybe he's just looking at Jalen in that way. That would make more sense.

I certainly look at him like that.

It occurs to me that there is one good thing in my life that didn't come with any nasty strings. One *amazing* thing.

Jalen.

I try not to stare at him as he flirts shamelessly with Andreas. I'm not mad about it. He's been saying forever that we both need Daddies to take care of us, and I bet Andreas would be a wonderful one for Jalen. I'll just be sad when he eventually moves on with his life. Devastated, actually, but it can't be helped.

Jalen would never want to be with a shy little mouse like me. We're just friends. *Best* friends. I'm not exaggerating when I say that he's the reason I've made it this far in life. I love him to the moon and back. But I know we're only friends. He's far too fabulous to be interested in me. No, I'm like his little brother, and that's okay.

However, I can't deny that I'll miss him whenever he moves on. I didn't think it would be for a while, but watching the way he and Andreas have been bantering back and forth over dinner has made me wonder if it could be sooner rather than later.

Jealousy isn't a useful emotion in my experience. It's okay to be sad or disappointed or to wish for something better for yourself. But jealousy is just mean-spirited. And yet when I look at Andreas laughing at Jalen's silliness, I can't help but feel a pang of something that might be akin to envy.

Anyone with eyes can see that Andreas is gorgeous. I compared him to Idris Elba before when Jalen and I were quickly getting changed back home. Jay insisted that Andreas is more of a James Bond in his fancy clothes with that English accent, but I pointed out that Idris Elba has been rumored to play the next Bond for years, so technically, we're both right.

But we can't both have him.

Not that *either* of us is trying to 'have' him, for crying out loud. But he's taken us to a swanky restaurant in the city, and if it was just two of us instead of three, I'd think it was a date.

No guy is ever going to pick me over Jalen, though. So even if this really is just some random night and we never see each other again, I can't be resentful if Andreas gives Jalen more attention than me. I want to see my bestie happy.

I just wish I could make him happy.

They're currently debating the merits of the infamous body swap episode versus the time travel one. I sip my drink and watch them like it's a tennis match.

"I love the one where Osh and Mina get stuck in the cave."

They both stop talking and look at me. It's then that I realize it was me who spoke.

"Oh, um, I mean…"

"That's a beautiful one," Andreas says.

He slips his hand over mine, and I swear my heart skips a beat. The older man's smile is like Christmas tree lights, shining just for me. Except that's crazy, and I know it. He's simply indulging a couple of lost souls for an evening. We're superfans of the same TV show, having a wander down memory lane. There's nothing more to it than that.

Right?

It's not long before I'm questioning myself, though.

I don't know how long we've been sitting at the table chatting, drinking, and laughing. But eventually, Andreas looks around and realizes that we're the only people left in the restaurant who aren't staff.

"Damn it, is that the time?" he says incredulously, looking at his watch. "They must hate us."

"After all the delicious food and drink we ordered?" Jalen says with a scoff. "I bet they love us."

He's got a point. I'm bursting at the seams after such a lavish dinner, and we've already had several things boxed up so we can take them home with us for lunch tomorrow. So it's not like we've been taking the piss.

But as Andreas calls our patient waitress over to ask for the bill, I can't help but feel some of my earlier worries sneaking back in. He's right. It is really late. I'm not sure if our train will still be running to get home, and even if it is, I don't like getting it late on the weekend with all the drunks.

"Hey, are you okay?"

I look up to see Jalen regarding me in concern. *Oh, no.* I must have been chewing my lip. I do that when I get anxious.

"Uh, yeah," I say quietly as Andreas is busy very kindly paying for our meal. I'm not certain, but from the look on the waitress's face, I think he's giving her a really big tip. That makes my heart swell. He's so kind.

But now it's time for us to say goodbye. So long as we can actually *make* it home.

"I'm not sure about the train times. We should look."

Jalen blinks at me. "Oh, boo-boo. Didn't you hear Andreas saying a while ago that he's going to order us a taxi and not to worry? My poor baby."

Even though that's incredibly extravagant, relief rushes through me. "What, really? That's so nice."

Andreas finishes getting his card back from the waitress, and she walks off to go get us our doggy bags. He shakes his head. "Actually, I was thinking about that."

My heart drops. I knew it was too good to be true. No, it was too *greedy.* Between the action figures and dinner, he's been ridiculously generous tonight. He can't pay for our taxi as well.

"It's okay," I assure him. "I'm sure we've still got time to make the last train if we hurry."

He frowns at me for a second before his expression melts. He reaches out and doesn't just place his hand over mine this time. He links our fingers together and rubs his thumb against my skin. "Oh, no, sweetheart. That's not what I meant. I'd be happy to pay for a taxi to get you both home safe and sound, but, um…I've had another crazy idea."

I don't really understand where he's going with this. I'm still buzzing from the champers and feeling anxious that we've overstepped. "Um, okay," I say with a nervous giggle.

Andreas glances at Jalen, but Jalen lifts his eyebrows in confusion. I don't think he knows what's happening either.

"Do either of you have work tomorrow?"

It's my turn to look at Jalen. "I don't, no," I say. My shifts are totally randomly assigned each week. It's one of the things I hate most about my job. But for once, luck is on my side. I don't have work again until ten o'clock on Sunday morning.

"Not me," Jalen says with considerably more excitement. "Not until Monday." I'm too nervous trying to imagine what Andreas is about to suggest.

He licks his lips and glances at Jalen again. Oh, no. Is this where he asks Jalen to stay and puts me in a taxi? If he does, that will be *fine!* I make myself promise that I'll be happy for my friend.

"I've really enjoyed entertaining you both tonight," Andreas says. "It's been my pleasure. So…I didn't know if perhaps you wanted to stay at my place tonight instead of trekking it all the way back to Mount Druitt. I've got a spare room and a sofa," he adds hastily, clarifying what he means by 'stay over.' "And then tomorrow, I thought it might be fun to go shopping for Christmas decorations for you guys. I couldn't help but notice that your place doesn't have any and, well, I really like the thought of doing that for you. But only if you think it would be fun."

When I remember to breathe again, I realize that he's nervous. *He's* nervous asking if he can spoil us with a Christmas shopping spree.

I'm so overwhelmed I could cry. Christmas with my family was always awful, but every year, I got my stupid hopes up that *this year* it would be like you see in the movies. I so wanted my first holiday season with Jalen to be special, but we were too poor to do much about it.

Andreas winces. "It's too much, isn't it? I'm sorry. I'll order you a cab. I never meant to make you feel—"

"NO!"

It takes me a second to realize once again it's me who's spoken. I clear my throat. I might be overwhelmed and still not really sure why this man is being so impossibly kind, but I love Jalen too much to let this opportunity slip by. He left his whole family back in California to come live with me. To save me. He deserves everything. So I can accept Andreas's magical offer if I'm doing it to give my best friend a little Christmas miracle.

"That sounds amazing," I say, trying not to get emotional. I squeeze Andreas's hand which is still entwined with mine. "Doesn't it, Jay?"

Jalen's mouth is hanging open. But he seems to notice that I've said yes, and suddenly breaks into a brilliant smile. "It sounds sugary sweet, Daddy-O," he says, clapping his hands like a little kid. His choice of words seems a bit odd, but then again, he's often coming out with Americanisms that surprise me.

Andreas looks between us with relief clear on his face. "Yeah? Not too much?"

"Just right," I tell him earnestly.

My parents hated fun. They had no sense of adventure. And I won't lie, the thought of doing something this wild would have most likely scared me senseless if I were sober. But I've had just enough Champagne to throw caution to the wind. Why not let a handsome man treat us? Just because I don't understand why he'd be so kind to someone like me, I can easily see how he'd be dazzled by Jalen.

And we'll be together, Jalen and I, so we can look after each other. I'm pretty sure this guy isn't a madman, but if he gets dodgy, Jalen will take care of me.

Besides, I can't go around thinking all strangers are out to get me, and I *especially* can't keep thinking that any man who shows even the slightest kindness to me is some sort of pervert. That's my mother talking, and she doesn't get a say anymore.

No. I'm going to take a leap and go stay at Andreas's place with my best friend and then maybe go buy a tree and some ornaments tomorrow. That sounds unbelievably wonderful.

I'm sure Andreas sees us as some sort of charity case. Or he really is trying to get with Jalen. Either way, I need to stop worrying about every little thing and do what Jay says. I need to have more fun, even if I don't believe I'm lucky enough to deserve it.

It's just one night, and then probably only tomorrow morning. How much trouble can we really get into?

CHAPTER 5

Jalen

Is it silly that I'm proud of Andreas? It's probably totally silly. But, girl, I can't help it!

Even though it surprised me, it's easy to see how clueless this guy is about being a deliciously hot Daddy, let alone that what he's been doing is sugar Daddying 101. He was so cute the way he stared at me when I explained it all at dinner.

But now it's like this lightbulb has gone off for him, I swear. I get why he kept looking at me when he suggested us staying over so he could take us shopping. It's as if he was checking in to see if he was doing it right. I feel like I've given him an assignment and he's determined to get an A-plus.

I would have hesitated if Colby hadn't been on board, but my little baby also surprised me by taking a chance to have some frigging fun. Good. He deserves someone like Andreas.

I know at some point, I'm going to need to step aside and give them both some room, but Colby isn't quite ready for that yet. He needs a little more handholding. Hell! So does Andreas. But that's cool. I can be their Yoda for a while and guide them through this whole thing.

Secretly, I was hoping Andreas might want to hang out with us again. I hadn't expected him to offer a sleepover, but now that the shock has worn off, I am ALL IN. His place isn't that far away from the Thai restaurant, but he still orders us an Uber anyway, probably because by the time we make it outside, Colby is swaying on his feet. My little sweetie isn't used to so much excitement, and he's all tuckered out.

When the car arrives, Andreas sits in the front and makes small talk with the driver. I bundle Colby into the back with me and sit him in the middle seat so we can snuggle. He rests his head on my chest, and I feel his warm breath ghosting over my skin.

I try to ignore the way it makes my insides clench. It's nothing new, after all. So I do what I usually do and act like it's nothing. It's easy to slip my hand against his and rest my cheek on top of his soft hair. For now, he's still mine to love and protect, even though I'm not very good at it.

If I have to let my baby boy go, it'll hurt less if it's to someone like Andreas. That's maybe a ridiculous idea, seeing as we all just met, but I can already tell he's kind, generous, and attentive. Colby needs a Daddy like that.

My needs are secondary. Besides, I know I'm a glitter-coated handful. It's probably going to take me a lot longer to find a guy willing to put up with my shrieking tantrums when I can't find my favorite lip gloss or the other half of a pair of shoes. Those kinds of dramas happen all the time with me. I'm so disorganized. I'm going to need an extremely patient Daddy, and I know they don't grow on trees.

Anyway, I'm racing ahead of myself, as always. Andreas didn't even realize he was being a sugar Daddy until I pointed it out. Now he appears to just be trying it on for size, and that's, like, totally fine. In fact, I'm here to be his biggest cheerleader—little skirt, pom-poms and all. I meant what I said at dinner. He might have had a preconception that it's some kind of seedy thing, but I truly believe that it can be a very wholesome and fulfilling kink.

I mean, all you have to do is just look at the way he's beaming as he rushes around the car to open the door for us when we arrive in front of his apartment building. He's absolutely loving spoiling the two little lost lambs he's stumbled upon. And I very much like being spoiled.

But I love seeing Colby happy even more.

Not for the first time (even that day), I mentally cuss out his awful family. How could they just let him go and forget about him like he's nothing? He's *everything*. Bigoted meanies. Well, hopefully, Colby will meet the perfect Daddy and then he'll be the one forgetting all about his stupid family instead.

"Thank you," I purr as Andreas gives me his hand to help me out of the Uber. Colby blushes when Andreas does the same for him. Andreas thanks the driver and takes a second on his phone, presumably giving him a rating. Then he uses a key fob to let us inside the building.

It's so fancy it even has a concierge. Instead of heading straight to the elevators, Andreas takes a detour over to the guy working the night shift behind the desk.

"Hey, Arnold," he says cheerfully. "I think I just had a bag of groceries delivered?"

The guy smiles and reaches down to his feet. "You certainly did, Mr. Lau. Here you go. Have a nice night."

"You, too," Andreas says, giving him that gorgeous smile of his. He holds the bags up as he approaches us, guiding us toward the elevator. "I grabbed you both toothbrushes as well as some nice things for breakfast."

Okay, even my cold heart melts a little. How can he be so thoughtful?

"Oh, good. Now neither of you will have to deal with my morning breath," I say instead, making them laugh.

The ride up doesn't take that long since the building isn't

that tall, but it's still a hundred times better than our place in every way. I marvel at the plush carpets and fancy light fixtures in the hallway, wondering what Andreas's apartment is going to look like. Being a graphic designer, he must have great taste.

If he does, I'm going to have to wait a little longer to find out. Or perhaps I never will. His home is disappointingly bare. Don't get me wrong, it's fab-you-lous. All open plan with a shiny kitchen and a view from his wrap-around balcony that probably lets you see all the way to Sydney Harbour in the daytime. But there's just no real evidence of a personality. The only thing I see is what looks like a reasonably big family photo on a side table in the living room. The rest just kind of feels like a display home.

He must sense my surprise, since he rubs the back of his neck and looks around sheepishly. "I'm not used to having guests," he admits.

"It's lovely," Colby says immediately, sounding almost defensive. My heart swells. He's too cute.

But Andreas shakes his head. "It's boring," he says. "I spend too much time at work. Part of my plan for taking this time off was to do some decorating, but you guys beat me to it."

I realize he doesn't have any Christmas decorations up, either. He might want to take us shopping for some tomorrow, but I'm going to bully him into getting some for himself as well.

"Oh, honey," I say with a snap of my fingers. "It just needs a little TLC. Can we check out the balcony?"

I grab Colby's hand and give Andreas pleading eyes. My intent was to make him laugh and forget about being self-conscious, and I'm thrilled to succeed. Yeah, the apartment is in dire need of a personality, but that doesn't detract from the fact that it's utterly *stunning*. You could decorate our place till the cows come home, and it would still be falling apart.

"Go for it," Andreas says. He points at the door. "You'll need to turn the key to get out, though."

"Girl, who are you expecting to rob you? Spider-Man?" I joke as I drag a giggling Colby over to the patio door and let us out.

Andreas's chuckles follow us into the lovely warm evening. Even in the dark it's a wonderful view. The harbor and Opera House are somewhere to the right of us and Manly Beach to the left. Lights twinkle from the houses on both sides of the water where small white boats bob, waiting to go out again the next day. The balcony is huge, and Andreas has a whole-ass sectional out here, so I pull Colby to sit down with me.

"Are you okay?" I whisper.

He blinks his pretty blue eyes and looks up at me from where I've tucked him under my arm.

"Me? Yeah. Why?"

I use my hand to indicate Andreas's apartment. "This is a lot."

He nibbles his lip, and I curse myself. I don't want to put doubt in his mind, but at the same time, I have to check in that he's actually all right and not just going along with my harebrained scheme.

"Yeah, but…it's fun, right?" he says timidly.

I nod, trying to convey my enthusiasm without over-whelming him. "So fun! And Andreas is super nice. I just… well, you're my boo and I wanted to double check you were having fun."

He glances back through the glass door, and I do as well. Andreas looks to be puttering around in the kitchen. Prob-ably putting our leftovers in the fridge and sorting out those groceries he bought.

When I look back, Colby appears thoughtful. But then he smiles at me. "It's like you said. Andreas can afford it, and we're not being greedy. I wonder if he's maybe a bit…well, a bit lonely. Don't you think?"

I brush a lock of Colby's sandy blond hair back, my heart aching for him and how selfless he is. "I think you could be right. Andreas seems to want to spoil someone, so why not us? It's nice to meet a fellow JG nerd, after all."

"Right?" Colby agrees enthusiastically. "Especially one so *hot.*"

We burst out laughing and don't stop until Andreas joins us on the balcony with a tray of glasses filled with water. "Everything good?" he asks with a crooked eyebrow.

I grin as I manage to calm myself down, gratefully taking the drink he offers. I like being a bit drunk, but I don't want to wake up with a headache. "It's great, D-Andreas."

Wow. I know I've had Champagne, but the temptation to call him 'Daddy' was *strong* just then. SERIOUSLY, though! I can't help it. He's got Daddy vibes rolling off him in every direction. *Urgh,* he makes me want to be such a naughty brat but at the same time be so good for him. I want him to be proud of me.

But that might be taking something away from Colby, and I'd never do that. I need to at least give him a chance to see if anything's blooming between him and Andreas before I do anything stupid.

Andreas gives me a knowing smile, which makes me think he caught my almost slip up. But seeing as I was the one who encouraged him to try out the whole sugar Daddy thing, then teased him as we left the restaurant, I'm hoping he doesn't actually mind.

There's no denying this whole thing is very unusual and happening extremely fast. Six hours ago, I was sulking because I thought I'd lost the Jurassic Galaxy set to a stranger. Now Colby and I are sharing the gift I so desperately wanted for him, and we're here getting to know its previous owner.

Not just getting to know. I feel like we're already becoming friends. I think Colby's right. Andreas seems like he needs a better work/life balance, and who better to give that to him than two little cuties like me and my bestest friend in the whole wide world?

After making sure we've both drunk enough water, Andreas juts his chin back toward the apartment. "So, who wants the spare room and who wants the sofa-bed? I promise both are pretty comfortable, and I've got plenty of spare bedding to go around from when my sister and her kids visited a couple of years ago."

I glance at Colby to find him already looking at me, waiting for me to take the lead. I promised to look after him and keep him close. Sleeping in a stranger's house—even one as nice as Andreas's—does come with certain risks and will certainly leave whoever's out on the couch feeling exposed.

Dang it. If I'm going to lose Colby sooner rather than later, I'm going to take what I can of him now, while I still have the chance.

"Actually, can we share the spare bedroom?"

I watch Colby for his reaction, and he smiles at me with a little nod.

If Andreas is taken aback by my request, he doesn't show it. He just pauses a second before smiling broadly. "Of course. No problem at all. Let me show you where it is and make sure you've got all you need. I have my en suite, so feel free to use the main bathroom as much as you like."

I love the way he fusses over us as he herds us into the second bedroom and shows us how he's bought us each a toothbrush. He's also found two of his T-shirts that we can wear with our underwear to sleep in.

What really squeezes my heart, though, is that he thought to order me makeup remover wipes and moisturizer from the grocery store. He tries to play it cool by saying his sister drilled it into him how you should never sleep in your makeup, but that's honestly one of the most thoughtful things anyone's ever done for me, and for once, I find myself struggling for words.

He bids us good night, and Colby and I work naturally around each other to get ready to sleep. When we eventually slip under the covers, Colby automatically nuzzles against me to spoon. We've shared beds several times since I arrived in Australia, so it's no big deal. Or so I tell myself.

Colby seems to fall asleep quickly, but I find myself staring at the walls for a long time before I drift off. My head is full of thoughts of my best friend as much as my new friend, and I'm really not sure what to do or how to feel.

But eventually, I soothe myself with the knowledge that everything will be simpler in the warm light of day. We're all just having some fun. No need to overanalyze it.

We'll probably have forgotten all about it once the new year rolls around. It'll just be a crazy story that Colby and I reminisce on from time to time.

Except one last thought slips in just before I lose consciousness. Maybe Andreas and Colby will be a couple by the time we're singing Auld Lang Syne.

Where will that leave me?

CHAPTER 6

Andreas

When I wake up and my first thought is *have you gone insane?* I make a decision. Carpe diem. Seize the day.

Yes, when I woke up yesterday, I was excited about delivering the toy set and had no idea where the afternoon would lead me. But do I regret it?

Absolutely not.

It was the most fun I've had in a hell of a long time. Probably the most human interaction I've had in months outside of colleagues, as well. Sure, we socialize with after-work drinks and karaoke and the like. And I have my rock-climbing buddies. However, I've recently realized how easy it is to be alone in a crowd. How easy it is to get lost.

Jalen saw straight through the bullshit and got right to the heart of me in a matter of hours. I must admit that before I fell asleep, I did a little online research, and it looks like he's definitely onto something with this sugar Daddy business. It can manifest in many different ways, but he was correct that it comes down to a kink that thrives on a specific kind of financial arrangement.

The idea of spending the day spoiling those two sweet

boys with a whole load of decorations for their tiny flat makes me feel like Father bloody Christmas. I'm hoping there'll be a chance for me to buy them lunch and maybe other treats as well.

And all I want in return is to see them happy. If they're enjoying themselves, that's all I need. If that's what it means to be a sugar Daddy, then sign me up.

I can see how I wouldn't want to be taken for granted, though. That would leave a sour taste. I'm not a walking credit card. But even after less than a day, I feel very confident that's not what either of these boys are about.

The other annoying voice in my head is nagging at me that it's a little weird that I've taken *two* young men under my wing. But weird by whose standards? Who here is actually judging me? Myself, and again, I decide that I don't care. As far as I'm concerned, Jalen and Colby come as a pair, and it would be unethical to separate them. Like bonded puppies.

As I take a quick shower, I keep arguing with myself. We're all consenting adults here, and all we're doing is being friends. If someone looking in from the outside thinks the dynamic is strange, that's their problem.

What I know is that when I let all the other bullshit fall away and just think about those sweet boys currently asleep in my spare bedroom, I get butterflies in my stomach and a deep feeling of contentment settles over me. I *know* I can look after them. That's my only job for today.

As I exit my bedroom, I'm pleased that I appear to have risen before them. They might be awake, but there's no movement in the apartment as I make my way into the kitchen and get the kettle boiling for tea or coffee. Once that's going, I nip back into the bedroom to retrieve the last surprise I snuck in from the grocery store order last night.

I didn't think the boys would want to spend all of today in the clothes they wore to dinner last night. I couldn't exactly get them whole new outfits—that would be a bit much to buy them *underwear* within hours of meeting them. But I could at least do this one thing.

As I lay out my spoils on the sofa, I grin. The boys will see them as they come out of their room. Then I get to work on breakfast. I ordered a mixture of pastries and fruit from the store that I can plate up now. But I also mix eggs together and get bread ready to toast once they're awake if they want hot stuff.

I don't have to wait long. Even though I'm trying to be quiet, I guess me moving around the kitchen still creates a certain amount of noise. My head whips around as soon as I hear the door creak open, and my heart melts as two sleepy boys emerge wearing my T-shirts over their underwear.

"Good morning," I say cheerfully as Colby rubs his eyes sweetly and Jalen yawns with a big stretch of his arms. "Did you sleep okay?"

"Like a log!" Colby declares.

Jalen shakes himself out before grinning at me. "Yeah, that mattress is amazing."

I beam, happy that I was able to take care of them even as they slept. This sugar Daddy thing is getting addictive fast. "Are you hungry? I know we had a lot to eat last night, but we've got a busy day ahead of us."

"Oh, wow," Colby says as he comes to inspect everything. "You didn't have to do all this."

I try and hide a laugh as Jalen elbows his best friend. "Say 'thank you, Andreas.'"

Colby rolls his eyes but then gives me a shy smile that makes my stomach flip. "Thank you, Andreas."

I wonder what it would be like if they called me 'Daddy.' That's what Google said last night was the norm. I thought it might be a bit weird. Seedy. But like my other preconceptions, it's not at all. In fact, I think I might love it. I swear

Jalen almost called me it when we got back here last night, but I couldn't be sure.

We are so far away from anything like that, though, so instead, I busy myself with the food and push those thoughts aside.

"Would you like eggs, bacon, and toast?"

"Ooh, yes, please," Jalen says as Colby nods with the same shy smile.

It seems they were distracted by me when they left the bedroom, so I jut my chin toward the sofa. "I got you both a present for today. You have to fight it out who gets what, though."

They frown comically before turning around. Colby gasps, and Jalen squeals.

"You bought us ugly Christmas sweaters?" he cries in delight as he claps his hands and skips over to the couch. Colby laughs as he takes the designs in. I got lucky that the store I ordered from actually had a decent selection.

One is black, white, and pink with a pattern of unicorns and snowflakes and the words 'I came to sleigh.' The other is covered with cats and actual little bells that tinkle. I'm not surprised as Jalen lunges for the unicorns, and Colby cries "Kitties!" The satisfaction I feel from nailing the gifts is slightly ridiculous.

"Don't you have one?" Jalen asks as he hugs his jumper to his chest.

I scoff and flip the bacon with a grin. "I have several. But I already know I'm going to wear the one with Father Christmas riding a T-Rex." The boys cheer and I grin even harder. Damn. I don't think I bothered to wear any of them last year except maybe to a silly work event. It feels really nice to have someone to dress up for, even if it is only in a novelty jumper.

It still throws me that this is the height of summer, and

actually Christmas T-shirts would be more appropriate. But I figure that we'll be indoors most of the day with air conditioning blasting, so the jumpers will be okay. For a moment, I get a rare pang of homesickness. Of course I miss my family, even if we do manage regular video calls despite the time difference. But there's nothing quite like bundling up for a chilly white Christmas, even if I love the beaches here.

As soon as it came, the moment of melancholy slips away. The whole point of today is to be in the here and now and stop worrying about everything else. This is about three people enjoying each other's company and getting into the Christmas spirit.

The two young men eat a surprising amount of breakfast, but that makes me happy. We can't take the leftover Thai with us, and I'm not sure when we'll be able to stop for lunch. So I'm glad I know they're fueled up to start the day.

They take turns in the bathroom freshening up. Colby is comfortable enough in his jeans from the night before, but Jalen's fancy pants are maybe not the best idea. I'm relieved I'm able to offer him some drawstring shorts that just about fit on his slim hips. He looks a little like a kid wearing his big brother's hand-me-downs, but the effect is so cute I tell him truthfully that he looks fabulous. He's got such confidence that he puts his heeled boots and lip gloss on and works it anyway.

We hit up the Big W department store across the bay in central Sydney and begin by looking at plastic trees. I miss having the real trees I grew up with, but it's obvious that they aren't practical down under, and to be honest a pine-scented diffuser brings back almost as much nostalgia for me.

After fretting over my empty apartment, I explain to the boys that I've got my own decorations in storage that I promise to get out as soon as possible. Today is about them and them only, and they should just go have fun picking out whatever they want. I can't, however, help but laugh as Jalen runs straight over to a white tree with pink LED tips.

"Okay, okay," I say after seeing Colby chewing his lip anxiously. "How about a compromise?" I sense he might want something a little more traditional.

Sure enough, we soon stumble upon a green plastic tree with multicolored LED tips that delights both the boys. From a practical standpoint, I approve that they won't have to faff around with separate lights, so we get right to picking out some tinsel and ornaments.

We agree on a pack of baubles, a set of sparkling icicles and snowflakes, and some fake candy canes. The way Jalen's eyes lit up makes me want to find some actual festive sweets for the boys to indulge in. After that, I steer them toward the wall of individual decorations, telling them they can each pick five.

"Five?" Colby says, sounding worried. He's so sweet.

I step closer to him and gently place my hand on his back, waiting to see if he has a problem with that. But if anything, he leans into the touch, and my heart aches.

"It's a big tree," I explain. "You'll be surprised how many decorations it can hold. And you want it to have personality, don't you? Not like my bloody place."

He giggles and looks up at me with shining eyes. "We can fix your apartment next."

"Exactly," I agree with a nod. "But today, we're focusing on your tree. Don't feel any pressure to get five if you don't find ones that speak to you. Let's say you can go up to five."

"Oops."

Colby and I look over at Jalen, who has his arms already full of various baubles.

"I can put some back," he says sheepishly.

I drop my head back and laugh. "Maybe take a look at them again and see which ones truly spark joy."

"They all do! It's Christmas!" He flutters his eyelashes at me, but I just arch my eyebrow at him until he sighs. "Fine," he grumbles.

I suspect that he actually enjoys the discipline. I read online that's what good Daddies do, anyway. I never want to be a hard arse, but part of being a Daddy is knowing what's best.

Besides, I know he's not being greedy. He's just excited by the glitter and bright colors.

"Andreas?"

I look over to see Colby carefully holding a very pretty fairy. "Yeah, hun?"

He nibbles on his lip. He does that a lot.

I try very hard not to think about how he needs someone to kiss it better.

"Do you promise?"

"Promise what?" I ask him.

He glances at Jalen, who's paused in his ornament selection to watch his best friend. "Do you promise that we can help you decorate your apartment some other time?"

My chest feels like it wants to explode. I was trying not to think about letting them go tonight without seeming too smothering and asking for their numbers or when I could see them again. But if Colby's already bringing up a perfect opportunity...

"I'd love that," I tell them warmly. I'm sure they both let out a small breath of relief, but maybe that's just wishful thinking.

"I'd love that, too," Colby says in a slightly shaky voice.

"Yes!" Jalen cries with a finger snap that almost causes him to drop all his remaining ornaments. "An-*dre*-as," he pleads, giving me puppy eyes. "Come help me decide, okay?"

I laugh, getting in between the two boys, discussing the

various merits of their choices until we're down to ten special baubles.

I want to give them boundaries because I can already see how that makes them thrive. But I kind of also want to hammer into them that they don't have to choose, not really. Life's too short. They can have whatever makes them happy, within reason.

That's certainly what I intend on doing.

CHAPTER 7

Colby

It's a few days later, and Andreas has kept his word. We're currently back in his beautiful apartment, carefully taking ornaments out of bubble wrap to hang them on his seven-foot-high tree. He's even got a little stepladder out for us to use.

Jalen and I are wearing the ugly sweaters he bought us as kind of a joke, but truth be told, I've been living in mine. Obviously not at my horrible job. I've got a polo shirt that I wear for a uniform, so the customers know who to yell at. But when I get home, I've been putting it straight back on.

A couple of times, I've even slept in it. Jalen doesn't know that. I'm too embarrassed to admit it out loud.

I can't help it, though. It's so completely alien to me to get thoughtful, spontaneous gifts. That's not to diminish all the wonderful presents Jalen's bought me over the years. He sent me things for Christmas and my birthday way before we ever met, and I know exactly what lengths he tried to go to this year to get me the best Christmas present. He's always thoughtful and wonderful.

But it's more to be expected to get gifts from your besties

at those times of the year. Andreas just got us these jumpers because he wanted to. Because they amused him, and he thought they'd make us laugh.

Somehow it's a different kind of gift.

It scares me how much I like it.

I'm not the kind of person who's popular and has people fawning over them. I saw it at school. How the popular girls got the most Valentine's Day cards and just sort of took it for granted because they were so beautiful. Don't get me wrong, a lot of them were pretty nice as well. But they accepted those gifts as if it was a perfectly normal thing to happen.

I'm sleeping in a jumper with literal bells on because I can't believe someone thought of me long enough to get me something special. Thoughtful. And that's not even taking the money he's spending into account.

I know it's not much to him, but thirty dollars on a joke gift is a hell of a lot to me. It means something.

So despite Jalen's many words of wisdom, I'm still struggling to accept the generosity a little. Even though we already had that amazing day with Andreas when he bought us all the decorations, took us out to lunch, then drove us home so we could decorate our flat. We even swung by here first so we could pick up our feast of Thai leftovers. He also got us some wine even though he wasn't drinking because he had to drive home.

Now here we are, back again in his amazing home. He already invited us to stay over, so this time we knew to bring our own jarmas and a change of clothes for tomorrow. I'm aware that a lot has happened fast, but it's crazy how natural it feels. He obviously loves having us around, and he makes me feel all warm and fuzzy. He's promised once we've put the tree and other deccies up, we can watch a Christmas movie of our choosing with hot chocolate and popcorn.

It kind of feels like a dream.

"You're very quiet," Jalen says playfully. He's sipping on a mimosa and probably hanging up baubles at half the rate I am, but I don't care. We're both having a lot of fun in our own ways.

I glance around, even though I know Andreas has popped out to run an errand. It's just the two of us for a while, festive music playing in the background while twilight creeps in outside.

"I'm just thinking," I say with a shrug. But I give him a smile so he knows it's not bad thoughts. Complicated, maybe. But not bad.

"About Andreas?" he asks in a sing-song voice. I try not to blush.

"Uh, yeah. A bit. He's just very kind, is all."

Damnit. I've been promising myself over and over that it's okay to like the older man and to relish in his attention and enjoy his gifts. But I'm sure he fancies Jalen and is just inviting me to hang out to be nice. Nothing more. I can't let on to Jalen just how much I like him and everything he's doing. Because if they get together, I want them to be happy.

"Hmm," Jalen says, quirking an eyebrow. *Very* kind. And handsome. And rich."

I shove him, but not so hard that he's in danger of spilling his drink. "Behave," I mumble.

"Hey," he cries, scandalized, as if he always behaves. "I speak nothing but the truth."

I sigh. "Can *I* tell you the truth?"

His face becomes serious, and he reaches over to squeeze my arm. "Of course, sweetie. Always."

I toy with the glass hummingbird in my hands. It refracts rainbow light, and I've been trying to find the most perfect spot for it on the tree so it can be appreciated the best. Something so beautiful deserves to shine.

Much like Jalen.

"I know you like Andreas," I begin, but he cuts me off with a scoff.

"Yeah, girlfriend! He's a cutie. But you know he likes you, too. A *lot*."

I hum, not quite convinced. But I can't quite bring myself to come out and say that I'll step aside and Jay can have him, not when I don't know what's going on in the grand scheme of things. So I stick to a different kind of truth.

"I really like the way he makes me feel when he buys us presents and fusses over us," I say in a rush. I duck my eyes and run my fingers over the glass bird's wing instead.

But Jalen sighs sadly. It's such an unusual sound from him that it makes me look up. "You know that's kind of the point. Right, baby?"

I shake my head, not sure I'm following. "Point of what? I know people give gifts to be nice, but this seems a lot. I don't know if I should accept all this, even if I want to."

Jalen puts his drink down and wraps both his hands around my free one. "Okay, sweetie-pie. You know how we talked about needing Daddies to take care of us, yeah?"

I shake my head and laugh. "I know *you* told me that *you* think we both need Daddies. I'm not sure about the whole idea."

He lets go of me with one hand to wave it around dramatically. "Well, *get* sure about it, boo-boo. Because it's already happening. Look around."

I blink. "I mean…I guess Andreas is older than us. But he's not dating either of us!" *Is he?*

Jalen laughs. "No, silly. But being a Daddy is often just who a person is at their core. Andreas is a full-on Daddy, a sugary one at that."

My eyes widen. "A sugar Daddy? Isn't that like…um… being a…a…?"

Jalen bats his eyelashes at me, clearly amused at how flustered I've become. "Richard Gere in Pretty Woman?" he asks innocently, but I blush all the same. He laughs but also grabs my hand to kiss my fingers affectionately. "A bit, sweet pea. But you're not Julia Roberts. Although your legs are just as nice as hers."

I roll my eyes. "Be serious," I grumble. "Besides, if anyone has legs like a movie star, it's you."

"I am being serious," he insists. "You feel good getting spoiled, right?" I nod. "It's not something you're used to, and it feels nice. It reminds you that you are a very awesome human being who deserves great things."

"I wouldn't go that far," I say shyly. "But…yeah. It's nice."

"Well," Jalen says, picking his glass up again and tilting it my way like he's the conductor of an orchestra. "That same warm, gooey feeling you get from being taken care of? Andreas gets the exact same feeling from doing the care*taking*. So no more worrying about it or feeling guilty, okay? Think of it as doing him a favor."

He smirks and sips his OJ and champers while I frown and consider what he's said. It never occurred to me that Andreas would be getting something out of buying us these things. I thought he felt obliged because he's rich and we're poor. But the notion that it could be something that makes him feel as amazing as I did when I saw the ugly Christmas jumper…

Well. That puts a whole new spin on it.

It's like the Christmas decorations thing. I was happy to let him spoil us as soon as he promised that we could return the favor. I know we haven't bought him anything, but just helping him out and spending time together makes me feel like we're redressing the balance. I don't just want to take. I want to give. Even if what I—or *we*—give isn't worth the same financially.

Quality time is worth the same, and technically that's

free. Us choosing to spend our evening here might 'cost' Andreas the price of dinner or whatever, but I feel like what matters is that we want to be here for his company just like how he wanted to come to our cramped and dingy flat just to hang out with us.

I lick my lips and give Jalen a serious look that he half returns. "So it's really okay that I'm enjoying all this as much as I am? It doesn't make me a bad person?" It can't do if Jalen really thinks that Andreas is getting just as much out of giving as we are receiving.

I'm sure if I had tons of money, I'd love to give to charities and stuff. It makes sense.

Jay's shoulders sag. "Babe," he says patiently. "You don't have a bad bone in your body. Yes, I've been saying this all along. I think Andreas has been looking for a relationship like this. Maybe without even realizing but looking all the same. It's extremely fulfilling for him. Oh! I guess it's not so different from being a top or a bottom, right? If one person prefers a position over another it doesn't mean both parties aren't having a fun time. You get me?"

I blush. He's so casual when he talks about stuff like that. He's pansexual, and some of the things he's told me that he's gotten up to are super hot, but they also make me squirm with embarrassment. There was a kinky club in LA where he topped with other twinks but bottomed for Daddies and dykes with strap-ons. Lord, just thinking about those stories makes me in danger of getting hard, and he can never, ever know that.

I'm not just very vanilla, I'm also pitifully shy. I've only done *it* a few times, and some were better than others. But I've never found it to be as mind-blowing as Jalen seems to think it is. Maybe I'm just doing it wrong.

However, I guess he has a tiny point. I know that the idea of bottoming—of being submissive—is way more appealing to me. The prospect of taking charge—if that meant topping or whatever—makes me want to shrivel up.

But obviously, I don't think topping is bad. Because I'm looking for a top (in theory, at least).

And I like the *idea* of sex a lot. Just because my experience so far has been mediocre doesn't mean I'm not hoping for more. I've written more than a hundred naughty fanfictions over the years, mostly with my favorite character Buckets. I see myself a lot in him, so writing those stories was kind of like imagining myself doing those sexy things. Through him, I had a *lot* of fun.

It's one thing to picture those scenarios via words, though, and quite another to envision them in real life. But maybe one day, I could take a leaf out of Jalen's book and embrace my sexuality a little more.

Anyway, my thoughts have wandered off on a tangent. Back to the situation at hand.

I mull over the new frameworks Jalen has given me. If I put myself in Andreas's shoes now, I can see what's going on from his perspective. And it almost feels like just being myself could be a sort of gift for him. That by allowing him to spoil me, I'm fulfilling a need for him.

That feels kind of beautiful when I look at it like that.

Of course, Jalen knows he's a gift to anyone who encounters him. So perhaps I can borrow a bit of his confidence and truly trust that someone's enjoying being around me, and that's enough.

"Yeah, okay," I say, not wanting him to launch into another speech about sexy stuff. "Come on, then. Let's get this tree finished before Andreas gets back. Show him how much we appreciate his generosity."

Jalen beams. "That's the spirit! WOOHOO! It's Christmas, and this year she's going to be *fabulous*, darling!"

I finally decide on the perfect spot for the glass

hummingbird and secure her onto a branch where she twin-kles happily.

"I think this is going to be the best Christmas ever," I say.

My words might be soft and quiet, but for the first time ever, I think I believe them.

CHAPTER 8

Andreas

"SO WHO ARE THESE NEW MATES, THEN?" MY SISTER, ANISHA, narrows her eyes at me through the video call. She's holding her phone in one hand and a glass of red wine in the other.

I laugh as I make my way along the path. At this time of year, there's an eleven-hour difference due to daylight savings. So it's nine on Sunday morning for me, but it's ten o'clock Saturday night for her, and after what I assume is most of a bottle of wine, she's got her fighting gloves on.

"It's a funny story," I say with a shrug. "We like this old geeky TV show, and we all just sort of clicked."

Anisha giggles. Despite being five years older than me, she's never forgotten how to have fun. It's one of the reasons her awful husband, Gregory, walked out on her. He wanted someone who took life seriously. My sister has always argued that life's far too short to be taken seriously.

"Oh my god, was it that crazy space dragon one you were obsessed with?"

"Space *dinosaurs*, I'll have you know," I correct her with an arched eyebrow.

She laughs again. "My apologies. How could I make such

a heinous mistake? But aww, seriously, hun. I love that you're actually off out having fun for once. Normally when I call you, you're reading a book or riding your bike."

I give her a look only I, as her 'baby' brother, could get away with. "There's nothing wrong with either of those things," I inform her.

"Yes, but neither of those things have penises, either, darling," she says matter-of-factly, waving her wine glass at me.

I snort. "You want the girls to hear you talking like that?" I admonish.

It's her turn to blow a raspberry. "They're both at secondary school now. They know exactly what penises are and to not let any grotty boys put them in their bodies for several more years."

Realizing I'm never going to win a parenting argument with an actual parent, I shake my head. So long as my nieces are both safe and happy, that's all I care about. I feel grateful that Anisha loves them both enough for two parents, considering that her ex has run off with a woman half his age and now barely remembers his daughters' birthdays.

I, on the other hand, make sure to post their gifts a month in advance so they definitely arrive back in the UK in time.

It's moments like these I do wish I wasn't so far away. Life here in Sydney suits me so well. The climate, the people, the size of the city and all that. But I do miss my family. My parents are getting on a bit now as well. I do hate the special and not-so-special occasions I miss out on from being on the other side of the planet.

Speaking of which, my big sister isn't afraid to call me out. Again.

"So you still not coming home for Christmas this year?" she asks with a raised eyebrow, flicking her braids over her shoulder, an impressive move, considering both her hands are still full.

I sigh. "I'm sorry, sis. I really am. It just…didn't work out."

That's a lie, and we both know it. She just doesn't understand *why* I haven't come back for the holidays—or at all—since I emigrated. But the truth is kind of embarrassing. I made a promise to myself that I wouldn't go back until I met someone special. Someone to introduce them all to. Every year I think *next year,* and then that turns into this year and so on.

"Well, I suppose you'll spend it on the beach like usual, yeah? Lucky bastard."

She grins to show me she means it. Christmas in the sun really is great once you get used to it. I still get nostalgic when I see dark, snowy nights in holiday films and the like. But I know I am pretty blessed.

"I'm actually on my way to the beach now," I tell her. "That's what my friends and I are doing. One of them works shifts, so we thought we'd have a little early Christmas today."

She makes another squeaky noise and looks at me with big, wet eyes. "Babe, I love that. You go have a great time. Make some memories. Take photos and send them to me."

"I will," I promise.

"And get some dick!" she shouts a little too loudly before cackling and hanging up on me.

The path down to the beach has got a fair number of people on it, so I wince apologetically at those who are looking back at me. But a couple of young women toast me with their suntan lotion bottles and give a little cheer. So I just laugh and shake it off.

I think it's more that I wouldn't want Jalen and Colby to think that was my intention. I mean, *yes.* They are both gorgeous, and my heart races whenever I see them. But the whole point of this is to look after them, so I've been trying to keep my *unmentionables* unmentioned.

Except I had this dream the other night that they were kissing each other for me. Jalen was giggling and kept looking over to make sure I was watching.

"Do you like that, Daddy?" he'd asked.

When I woke up, I had no choice but to sort myself out. It didn't escape my attention that it's been a very long while since I came that hard and fast only from my own hand. But afterward in the shower I felt ashamed. I don't want to disrespect them like that.

So I won't. It's that simple. We're friends, and that's all.

It's not hard to find the boys once I get down to Manly Beach. It's pretty small and tucked out of the way compared to some other beaches nearby. But also Jalen is wearing a bright pink sarong over his zebra print Speedos with matching pink heart-shaped glasses that make him look like Malibu Barbie. I love it.

The other day I double-checked his pronouns with him as he wears a lot of feminine things, and I was worried I should be addressing him differently. He said any are good but masculine ones are fine as a default. He told me that men can be beautiful just like women, and I couldn't have agreed more. I still think he's brave for being his authentic self, though.

He has no fear as he waves at me with his whole arm. He doesn't care who's looking. Even Colby manages a smile and a little wiggle of his fingers.

There goes my heart again, racing off into the distance.

"How's your sister?" Colby asks. I'd sent them on ahead when she called so she and I could have a little catch up.

I plop onto the blanket they've laid on the warm sand. "Giving me grief for missing Christmas again," I say with a laugh that mostly manages to mask my guilt. "I promised her maybe next year."

Jalen sighs and cracks open an equally pink hand fan. "Yeah, my family was a little bit sad. But I only got here a few months ago. It's not like I have the money to fly back out again so soon. Like you say, I'll probably see them next year anyway."

I shrug. "It's not such a big deal. My family's used to it. Growing up, my mum had her brother in the UK, even if his family was a couple hours' drive away. But her parents and sister were all the way back in Jamaica. We hardly ever saw them. And my dad's family were mostly in Hong Kong until the territory was handed back to China in '97. A lot of them moved to England after that, so we saw a good deal more of each other, which was nice for both him and us."

Jalen tilts his head. "So you're half-Asian, half-Caribbean," he says.

Given that I'm pretty sure his family's of Mexican origin, I'm almost confident he's not going to say anything ignorant. But a lifetime of wariness still puts my teeth slightly on edge.

"And one hundred percent British, baby," I reply with a wink, hamming up my London accent.

That makes the boys laugh. Well, Jalen laughs loudly. Colby gives a little smile and traces his fingers through the sand.

Jalen playfully hits me with his closed fan. "All right, Austin Powers," he teases. "What I meant was, I bet the food in your house was *amazing* growing up."

I grin, partly relieved, partly because it was true. "God, I miss my dad's cooking," I say, shaking my head. "Mum could burn a boiled egg, but Dad mastered all of his mother-in-law's recipes he could squeeze out of her every time she visit-ed." I sigh, trying not to let melancholy creep in. "My nan passed about ten years ago. I always wished I could have had a bit more time with her."

Jalen reaches out and touches my arm. "I bet she was proud of you, though."

I drop my head back and laugh. "You have no idea. The aunties banned her from bragging about me sometime around 2008. It never did stop her, though."

"I bet the aunties still brag about you," Jalen says with a wink. It's an unusually tender moment with my little firecracker, and I can't help but cherish it.

I also can't help but notice that Colby is determinedly getting food and drinks out of the cooler for us, not joining in the conversation about our families at all. However, I feel like we've spent enough time together that I want to ask about his situation. I have a hunch he needs a little help healing from something.

Potentially a lot of help.

"Are your family close by?" I ask him.

He shrugs. "They're in Newcastle."

That's a couple of hours north of Sydney if I remember correctly. It cracks me up how many places here are named after towns back home in the UK.

"Colby's family is right here with him," Jalen says hotly, ignoring the bottle of juice his friend has in his hand as he throws his arms around him. Colby bites his lip, and pain slashes through my heart. "Fuck those guys," Jalen adds.

I'm almost certain that's the first time I've heard Jalen swear. He's colorful with his language but doesn't seem to enjoy cursing. The word hits like a harpoon.

I reach out and squeeze Colby's knee. "Are you not close with them, then?"

Colby takes in a shuddery breath. He smiles sweetly at Jalen before gently extracting himself from his embrace. "Not really, no."

"They sent Colby away for conversion therapy," Jalen hisses, tears glistening in his eyes. "They tried to make him pray the gay away. His dad used to—"

"My dad's not here now," Colby says firmly, and I can't help but feel proud of him.

Jalen's only defending him, and I love that. But today is supposed to be a celebration. A mini early Christmas. If Colby doesn't want to bring that stuff up, I respect that.

Colby grabs Jalen's hand and kisses his fingers, the way Jalen often does to him. "I chose to walk away," Colby says, his voice wavering, but his conviction seems strong. "I told them where I am. They can contact me anytime they want. But unless they stop seeing me as nothing but a sinner, rather than their son, I haven't got anything I want to say to them. And *that's okay.* I'd rather have Christmas on the beach with you a million times over. That's what you promised."

"I did," Jalen agrees.

They look into each other's eyes for long enough that I start to feel like I'm intruding. But then Colby shakes himself and turns back to me. He wipes his damp eyes, but he's also smiling. "Would you like to have Christmas Day on the beach with us as well, Andreas? You probably already have plans, but—"

"No, no," I say quickly. "Well, I was going to volunteer at the hospital, actually. But I can do both. My company donates presents to the children's ward, and I like to go give them out."

Jalen's face morphs in delight. "Oh my god. Do you wear a little Santa outfit?"

"No," I say, arching my eyebrow. "It's an elf, actually."

I'm making it up, but it gets the boys laughing all the same, and that's what I wanted after our serious conversation.

Although I'm grinning as I open up various boxes of food,

it has left me wondering something. If we're all alone on Christmas, that makes total sense to spend it together. Jalen and I can't be with our families, and Colby basically doesn't have one.

But I *do.* And I haven't seen most of them in over five years. Anisha came for that visit with the girls, but that was two-and-a-half years ago now.

What am I really waiting for? To share that experience with someone? Or…two someones. But that would be crazy, right? It's one thing to agree to spend the twenty-fifth together when we're all right here in the city. But am I really thinking what I think I'm thinking?

What I'm *thinking* is what's the use of having all this money if it just sits in the bank. I might have my apartment, but what else am I really doing with it? Investing it? Saving it for a rainy day?

The sun is most definitely shining right now, no rain in sight.

I decide to shove the idea to the side. Today we have food and sunscreen and wine and even a mini Bluetooth speaker to play some tunes on quietly, just for our little corner of the beach. The water is sparkling, and I'm spending more quality time with these two amazing young men who make me laugh as well as my heart soar.

If this is just our first picnic of many, I'll be entirely grateful to the universe for bringing us together. But I can't help but feel like having grown up with sunny Christmases all their lives, there might be another kind of holiday season I could show them.

I'm getting ahead of myself. Anisha said chances of snow this year back in the UK were minimal anyway, so I'm not really missing out on what's in my mind. Those kinds of Christmases only happen in films, anyway. It'll be dark and rainy, and we're here, basking on the beach.

Yet I can't let go of the idea that if I'm going to take this chance to try sugar Daddying, then I should go all in. Go crazy. Who knows how long this strange relationship between the three of us is going to last? They've said time and again that they wanted their first Christmas together in person to be as special as it could possibly be.

Why can't I give them a little Christmas miracle they'll never forget?

CHAPTER 9

Jalen

"I'm just *saying*," Colby 'just says' for the twentieth time. "Why's Andreas coming here? We always go to his place or into Sydney."

I shrug as I tip a bag of chips into a bowl. It's not exactly fine dining, but I wanted to have some snacks out for when Andreas arrives. I don't want to encourage Colby, but Andreas's sealed lips on his sudden, unexpected visit have got me a little nervous too.

"Maybe he's just conscious that we always travel to him," I say nonchalantly.

"Yeah, because his place is a hundred times nicer than ours," Colby argues back. "And there's nothing to do around here."

I sigh and walk over to where Colby's rearranging our now-beloved collection of Jurassic Galaxy action figures on the bookcase. I grip his shoulders so he'll look at me. *"We're* here. Andreas is coming to see us. He doesn't need a reason. He's our friend and he said he wanted to hang out."

Colby chews his lower lip. Not for the first time I want to

reach out and gently pull it out before running my thumb over it. But I know that's far too intimate for me to do.

"You're worried we're not good enough," I suggest.

His eyes go wide. "Me! I mean—I! *I'm* not good enough. You're always fabulous."

I huff and roll my eyes. "So are you, boo-boo. You don't need glitter to be fabulous, I promise. Just relax. This is no different from any other time we've hung out over the past few weeks." He arches an eyebrow at me. "Okay, *yes*," I relent. "It might feel just a teeny, tiny bit different. It's probably because it's so close to Christmas. Everything's a bit out of the ordinary right now."

One of the only good things about my boring job is that the office closes its doors around December twenty-first and doesn't open them again until at least January third. So I've just done my last day. Colby's schedule is horrible, but that can't be helped. At least he's only got two more shifts until we'll get a couple of days totally all to ourselves to celebrate the holiday.

Secretly, I'm hoping that Andreas might be coming over to surprise us with a fancy plan for Christmas Day. We already had our day-long picnic on the beach, after all. Don't get me wrong, I'll happily do that again. But I can admit that I am a little bit of a brat, and I wouldn't mind being swooped off my feet.

Again.

Andreas is just so fun. If it were any old guy throwing money at me and my bestie, the novelty would wear off pretty quickly, I know. It's sharing all this fun stuff *with* Andreas that's the best part.

The doorbell chimes, and I can't help but remember the first he rang it when I opened the door to find him standing there with a box full of goodies. I give Colby a little shake and a big smile. "It's fine," I assure him as I dash out into the hallway. "Everything's fine, buttercup!"

Andreas isn't holding anything this time, but his smile is just as bright as before. Possibly even better now that I've had the chance to get to know him so well. Either way, my heart does a little flip, and I melt against the doorframe.

"Hi," I say breathlessly.

He chuckles as he steps over the threshold, giving me a hug and kissing my cheek. All my queer friends say hello like that, so it doesn't really mean anything. Except my heart's forgotten that particular information and starts doing more gymnastics in my chest at the close contact.

"Hey, hun," he says. I love the way he says that in his London accent. It's so cute.

I regain my senses and step away so Colby can come over and get a hug as well. "Hi!" he says cheerfully. I can hear the nerves behind the one-syllable word. I wonder if Andreas knows Colby well enough yet to notice it, too.

There's a slightly awkward air as we all move into our tiny living room. Andreas takes the armchair, so I join Colby on the sofa. It's small but just big enough to accommodate the two of us comfortably.

The trouble is, despite all the time we've spent together recently, it suddenly feels like we're interviewing Andreas for a job. Not that I've ever done that, but the way we're facing each other and the tension we're all carrying makes it strange.

"Drinks!" I blurt out. "Shall I—I mean—Andreas, what would you like?"

He smiles warmly at me, and some of the tension fades away. "Lemonade would be great," he says.

"Me, too," Colby squeaks.

That's fine, but I'm fixing myself a damned mimosa.

I hurry back from the kitchen to find the other two stiltedly discussing the traffic on Andreas's drive over. I hate this. We've all been having such a wonderful time together, but something about this evening has made it go all off-kilter.

What am I expecting to happen here? That he's going to 'break up' with us? None of us are dating, and I was half expecting this to be a short-term thing anyway while he tried on his sugar Daddy legs for size. I shouldn't be anxious if this is goodbye.

But I am.

Once everyone has their drinks and I'm settled back on the couch, I decide to stop dancing around the issue. "Is everything okay?" I ask Andreas bluntly. "You're acting weird."

"Jay!" Colby gasps, but I keep my eyes on Andreas.

He looks sheepish but he also grins and shakes his head. "Yeah, you're right. I wanted to talk to you boys about something, but I'm aware it's a big thing that'll be kind of out of the blue." He sighs and rubs his hands together. "Okay, it might help if I tell you a bit about my friends back in London."

I raise my eyebrows. "You haven't mentioned any of them before," I comment.

"That's because I haven't spoken to most of them in over a decade," he retorts sadly. "Well, you know. There are always Facebook posts and happy birthdays and all that. But we haven't been *friends* in a long time."

I glance at Colby. We share a look before Colby—who's closer—reaches out and rests his hand on Andreas's knee. "I'm sorry."

He nods. "Me, too," he says with a rueful chuckle. He takes a minute to look at the Jurassic Galaxy figures, apparently collecting his thoughts. "They were all people I knew from school and uni, with a few people's other halves folded into the mix. It was a great bunch. But...things change when you're all sharing four-bedroom houses and barely making it through to the next payday…then one of you becomes an overnight millionaire."

I blink. Obviously, he told us the Snippet story early on to explain why he was more than able to spoil us the way he does. But I never thought about what his life was like before.

"Oh, wow," Colby says, glancing at me.

He's probably wondering what that situation would do to us, which is silly. Because if I got rich, I'd just share it all with him anyway. But that's not the same as having a big friendship group, and I know it.

"It was fun to start with," Andreas says wistfully. "I *loved* being able to pay for dinner or holiday accommodation or whatever. But then…it was as if they came to expect it. Like I was just their lucky pot of gold. I was never allowed to be sad or stressed because I was rich. I always had to host because I had my own place, and it was the nicest, but they never asked how I *was* anymore. They certainly never stayed around to clean up after the parties that were happening every single weekend." He puffs his cheeks out and looks back at us. "I know, right? Poor little rich boy."

I shake my head fervently. "They were using you."

He winces. "I genuinely don't think they meant to. But I was suddenly living a completely different kind of life to them, and the power imbalance was toxic. The only thing I can compare it to was when people in the group started getting married and especially when they started having kids. A gulf appeared between those guys and the ones who were still single. Not that having kids is toxic, of course. But suddenly, they didn't know how to relate to each other so much. I think maybe at that point, some of them started to realize why I wasn't around anymore, but by then, it was too late.

"When my company offered me the chance to move to

Australia, I jumped at it. I saw the opportunity to start fresh with new friends, and I thought it would be perfect. Except the thing is, it's kind of hard to make friends in your thirties. A lot of people already have their people."

"But what about your sporty friends?" Colby asks sweetly.

Andreas nods. "Oh, yeah. There are some great guys there. But I've never been to a single one of their houses. Never met up other than to go for drinks after a session. It's the same with work. I've got a lot of people I'm *friendly* with, but I haven't had *friends* for years." He takes a breath and looks at the two of us. "Until I met you both."

Something unfamiliar and fragile blossoms in my chest. I can't think of anything snarky to deflect the raw emotion, so for once, I don't try.

"Oh, wow," I say simply. I don't know why, really, but I feel proud. Honored.

Andreas continues. "I feel like I've gotten to know you two better in the past few weeks than I have anyone else during the entire time I've lived in Australia. I'm telling you all this because I'm about to propose something absolutely mental, and I wanted you to understand the reasoning behind it so you don't think I've actually lost my mind."

I laugh. Partly it's nerves and feeling overwhelmed by Andreas's kind words about us. But part of it is excitement. I like it when he suggests crazy ideas. Usually, they're awesome.

"Come on, girl," I cry, my heart pounding. "Don't keep us in suspense like this!"

Colby swats my knee. "Don't push," he warns.

But Andreas is grinning, even if there's perspiration on his brow. He takes a deep breath and drums his hands on his knees. "I'll start off by saying this is all refundable. But...I might have had a couple of glasses of red wine last night, thrown caution to the wind, and booked a flight back to the UK for Christmas."

I can't lie. My heart drops. "Oh," I say, trying to sound cheerful and failing miserably. "You're, um, going back home."

Without us.

He blinks, then something seems to click for him. He shakes his head and leans a little closer. "I booked *three* seats on that flight. I'm asking you both to come and spend Christmas with me and my family in England."

Time screeches to a halt. I'm vaguely aware that my jaw is hanging open. My ears are ringing. Colby's gripping my hand so tightly that my fingers are starting to tingle. I'm not sure who grabbed for who, but we're clinging to each other now like a life raft.

"You…how…what?" I manage to utter.

He's looking between us. "I had a shit ton of air miles," he says like he's trying to calm a wild animal. "They were going to expire, and I thought: why not? You guys kept saying you wanted this holiday to be special, and I figured you might enjoy a white Christmas. Or at least a gray one."

"You want us to fly around the world to spend Christmas with your family that you haven't seen in five years?" Colby asks in a strangled voice.

Andreas inhales slowly, then nods. "I know we only just met, but for the first time since I moved, I finally feel like I have family *here.* Our talk on the beach the other day made me realize I don't want to put off going back home yet another year, but I hated the idea of you both staying here by yourselves. So I want you to come with me. On an adventure."

The whistling in my ears suddenly breaks free through my mouth, and I'm squealing in unbelievable excitement.

"Madonna on a moon buggy! Are you *serious?* Really? You want to take us to *England?"*

The first hint of relief washes over his face. "I really, really do," he says.

I look at Colby, who's still very stunned. "LONDON!" I yell at him, shaking him by the shoulders.

"Actually, we'd only make a short stop in London," Andreas explains. "Then we'd go down to Brighton to my parents' house. They're hosting."

I shake my head faintly. "I have no idea where that is, but it sounds amazing."

"It's by the sea," he explains kindly.

Colby blinks like he's coming back to life. "By the sea? We'd still be able to go to the beach on Christmas Day?"

Andreas laughs. "I mean, Brighton Beach in the winter is mildly terrifying, but yeah. Sure. Whatever you boys want."

Colby's breathing heavily. I don't blame him. I feel dizzy. "Oh," he says, his expression suddenly falling. "What about my job? They'd never let me take time off over the holidays, let alone at such short notice."

"Quit," I say without even thinking. "Quit. Leave. Walk out. You hate it, and they treat you like dirt."

He bites his lip and looks back at me. He knows I'm not wrong. "But what about our rent?"

There's a pause where Andreas seems to be holding his breath before he shakes his head and lets it go. "I can cover that, sweetheart. If that's all that's stopping you from joining us on this trip, I can help."

I expect Colby to say he couldn't possibly accept such a generous offer, but he looks like he's thinking it over. "If I screw over my current job, they might give me a bad reference for my next one."

"Ah," I say. He has a point there.

We all frown for a minute before Andreas hums. "How

much does this job know about your personal life, Colby?" he asks gently.

He raises his eyebrows. "Pretty much nothing," he admits. "It's such a hostile environment they actively try to stop us from making friends."

"Excellent," Andreas declares before realizing what he's said. "I mean, excellent for our diabolical plan. Do you think that you can convince them that it's a family emergency?"

I watch Colby turn that over for a second. "Yeah," he says slowly. "One of the guys disappeared without warning over the summer because his mom got cancer. They let him come back once she was settled into her new chemo routine."

Personally, I think Colby should use this as an opportunity to walk away and never look back, but we can discuss that later. Right now, I just want to convince him that telling this little white lie for the sake of an adventure of a lifetime will totally be worth it.

"When's the flight booked for?" I ask Andreas.

He grins sheepishly. "Uh, tomorrow evening. We'd land in London early on the twenty-third."

"What's the best way to call in sick?" I ask Colby.

He shakes his head. "Email, definitely email."

I grab his phone from off the coffee table and thrust it into his hands. "Do it now before you can chicken out. Don't think. Just do."

"Jay, are you sure—?"

"Absolutely," I say with as much conviction as I can muster. "We are going to do something crazy because otherwise we'll regret it for the rest of our lives."

I look back at Andreas. When he holds out his hand to me, I take it with a squeeze.

Yes, this is CRAZY. But what he said about his old friends makes perfect sense to me. Colby and I have said all along that he seems lonely. He's been missing out on all these adventures he could have been having for so long. Why wait until next year to go home for Christmas or invite us to travel with him? Why not start living again *right now?*

I'm not letting Colby miss this chance.

If I'm honest, I'm not sure how I fit into all of this. I'm so determined now that Andreas is Colby's dream Daddy, and I'm going to get them together if it kills me. Selfishly, I don't want to miss out on this trip, either. But if push comes to shove, I'll always put Colby's needs before mine.

Even if that means breaking my own heart in the process.

"So…we're really doing this?" Colby asks tentatively, his phone held aloft in his hand.

I look at Andreas and nod, watching his face split into an ecstatic grin.

"We're doing this," he says firmly.

"WOOHOO!" I scream and punch the air. *"London, baby, yeah!"*

I have no idea what this trip is going to bring, but I'm determined to go along for the ride.

I just hope I don't get left behind, that's all.

CHAPTER 10

Andreas

My apartment is quiet as I go to get a drink of water. I've been tossing and turning for an hour, so I hope this might help me finally drift off. It's after midnight, and the boys are asleep in my spare room once again, except this time they each have a suitcase standing in my front hallway, and tomorrow we'll all be heading off to Sydney International Airport together.

I'm still pretty convinced that I'm crazy. That any moment now they're going to turn around and call me out on how bloody weird this is. But right now...everyone seems to be on board.

I puff out my cheeks before taking a sip of cold water, my head buzzing as I let my eyes roam around my darkened home. I meant everything I said to the boys this evening. It just took a while for me to realize why it had felt so easy and natural to fall into friendship with them.

They're the friends I never had.

But things are different now. Mainly because I'm in my late thirties, and that makes me a hell of a lot older and wiser than I was when I first came into this windfall. Like I said, I do have a lot of people I'm friendly with who are closer to my age. I'd like to consider them friends to a certain extent. But not close companions or the kinds of people I want to open my heart up to.

Jalen and Colby still have that youthful exuberance that I've missed for so long. And yeah, it fits in really well with the nurturing Daddy tendencies I now acknowledge I have.

All in all, I truly believe us coming together like we did was a case of being in just the right place at just the right time.

Why fight that? Why um and ah and adhere to some imaginary timescale that society says we have to stick to? After that talk on the beach, I suddenly and quite forcefully realized that I didn't actually want to delay another year before going back to see my family. But I also didn't want to leave my two new gorgeous friends behind on their own, either.

I'm so happy they agreed. I'm so pleased we were able to get Colby out of work. Jalen is off until the new year, like me, as well, so we're free.

Free to fly halfway around the world and see what'll happen.

That's the part that makes my mind go blank, I'll be honest. I'm not sure what I'm expecting to happen between us. Maybe nothing at all. Hopefully, we'll create some amazing memories. All I know is that I want to spend more time together. I'm prepared to sit back to a certain extent and let the chips fall where they may.

Because I've been on group holidays before and never had these kinds of worries about what was going on. It was just a bunch of mates doing something fun together. But with our age gap and the whole sugar Daddy thing, I am aware there are other factors at work. I'm not that much in denial.

When I think about these boys, I have a *lot* of feelings. Complicated, contradictory feelings that I'm not sure what to do with. Try as I might, I can't deny that I find them both extremely attractive nor that my body reacts to them when they're near.

It doesn't seem to be bothering me that there are two of them. Not once has a voice popped up in the back of my head saying that if I'm gravitating toward them, that I should pick just one. To me, that doesn't seem to be an issue. They're so naturally a pair. My little yin and yang of quiet versus explosive energy. Separating them just seems wrong.

Again, that probably should be an issue. That's not normal, right? But what's 'normal' anyway? Besides, I'm not planning on acting on any of these confusing urges. I swore to myself that I was going to look after these boys, and that doesn't involve taking advantage of them. I'm just a friend to them. A father figure. I'd never betray their trust.

So for now, I'm carefully folding those feelings away into a box. As with everything I've done since we met, I really don't have an ulterior motive other than taking care of them. They're mine to spoil.

And to protect, Jesus H. Christ.

Even just thinking about what I've gleaned regarding Colby's family makes me want to punch things. I'll be totally honest, coming out to my parents in the nineties wasn't exactly a walk in the park. I didn't 'look' gay, according to them. Not like the few queer celebrities on the telly who were either overtly fem or just flat-out drag queens. I think mostly they were simply fucking terrified that I was going to get AIDS and were trying to protect me but…yeah. There were a few tense years back then.

I feel incredibly grateful for how far they've come. Anisha has always been on my side, and now my nieces are my biggest advocates. Hell, they even got my mum watching UK

Drag Race and took her to London Pride this year where she wore a T-shirt that said 'Free grandma hugs!' I don't think she was prepared for how many people would take her up on that offer or how emotional it might get.

Because even in this day and age, some people's families still disown them for the supposed crime of being who they are.

There's no doubt in my mind that my family loves me unconditionally. It's part of what's made me pull my head out of my arse and make these plans to go back and see them this year. No one knows what's going to happen tomorrow, and enough time has passed. A catch-up is long overdue.

But Colby doesn't know he's unconditionally loved. In fact, he knows the opposite to be true. The idea of that sweet, special young man being sent away somewhere where they tried to drill it into him that he's somehow wrong or perverted or a sinner makes me sick to my stomach. And even though Colby stopped him from finishing his sentence, I'm almost certain that Jalen was trying to tell me that Colby's father was physically violent with him.

I curl my fist as I lean against the breakfast bar that separates the living room and kitchen spaces. I've never been an aggressive person beyond video games. But if I ever came face-to-face with that man, I'm not sure I'd be able to control myself.

Exhaling, I release my fist and center myself in the here and now. The past is done. The future is uncertain. All I can do is dedicate myself to the present with my whole heart. I'm going to give those two boys a trip they will never, ever forget.

Movement catches my eye, and I immediately stand up straight. But then I relax and smile as a sleepy Jalen emerges from the spare bedroom. I wait until he carefully closes the door before giving him a little wave.

"Hey," I whisper.

He rubs his eyes and pads over to the kitchen. He's wearing soft shorts and an off-the-shoulder cropped tee with rainbows all over them. "Thought you were asleep," he mumbles.

I chuckle as I go to fetch him some water. "Not yet. I was thinking over some things. Travel logistics," I lie, not wanting to worry him with talk about Colby's family.

He nods and accepts the drink that I assume he came out here for. He gulps some down before yawning and then blinking at me, like he's finally actually waking up. "I was asleep, but then I had a nightmare, and then I was just thinking all these things, and I couldn't get back to sleep, not really."

I tilt my head as I look at him. "I'm sorry, sweetheart. Anything you want to talk about?"

He rests his hip against the breakfast bar so he's facing me as he chews his lip. Then he places the water down and crosses his arms. I know it's the middle of the night, and I imagine neither of us wants to disturb Colby, but he's being unusually subdued. Normally, when he rouses in the morning, he does so with a marching band and confetti cannon in tow. Being sleepy shouldn't dampen his spirits this much.

Oh, no. Did I go too far with this trip suggestion, after all?

He opens and closes his mouth a couple of times. Then I'm horrified to realize that his eyes have filled with tears.

I move before I can think, enveloping him in my arms. "Jalen, what's wrong?" I hiss as he clings to me.

"I'm sorry," he squeaks quietly, his body shaking against me. "I don't want to be selfish. I really don't. But I really want to come on this trip! I'm so sorry."

I frown, not following. So I look back in order to look him in the eyes. They're glassy. and I take a second to brush the tears from his cheeks with my thumb.

"What are you talking about? Of course you're coming on the trip. Why are you sorry?"

He takes a couple of jagged breaths, his brows knitted together. "I don't want to get in the way."

Nope. No idea. "Of what?" I probe.

He looks away and tries to squirm out of my grasp, but I hold on to him. I can't say I've been particularly domineering in my previous relationships, but I can tell this is a Daddy thing, and it's hitting me hard and fast. I'm not letting him go until he tells me what's wrong so I can make it better.

Eventually, he relents. "I don't want to get in the way of you and Colby," he says miserably.

My stomach drops. "Oh, sweetheart," I say, hugging him against me once more. "That's not possible, I promise you."

"But you like him!" he shrieks, still managing to keep the noise down somehow. "And he likes you."

"And I like you as well," I say firmly. "A *lot*. Do you like me?"

He's the one to pull back this time and look at me like I just grew a second head. "Girl, what? Duh."

I laugh as relief flows through me. There's my boy.

"Jalen," I say patiently as I sweep a curl of his hair back from his face. His brown eyes are beautiful, and this close, I can see just how many freckles he has across his nose and cheeks. "I like you and Colby equally. I like you very much. That's why I invited you on this epic trip to visit my family. There is no either/or. Just both."

"But—" he begins.

I shake my head. "No buts. You're a package deal."

He seems to mull that over for a bit. "Oh," he says. "Okay."

I tilt my head. "Are you disappointed?"

"No!" he cries a little too loudly. After glancing at the closed bedroom door where Colby is asleep, he looks back at me. "No, not disappointed. But, well…I've been trying to get Colby a Daddy, and I thought you'd be a great one."

I chuckle and rub his back. His body feels so good in my arms. "You make it sound like you've been down the river fishing for one."

He rolls his eyes and pokes my shoulder.

"You mock my pain," he grumbles.

I shake my head again. "I promise I'm not," I say softly. "And I know you've been looking out for him for a long time. Jalen…you love him, don't you?"

"Psh," he says with a wave of his hand. "Of course I do. He's my ride-or-die bestiest bestie ever." I pin him with a serious look until he deflates slightly. *Mariah on a milk carton,* I love him so much," he says sadly. "But he doesn't need me. He needs a Daddy."

Poor baby. I rub his back a little more. "I think he needs you very much," I say truthfully.

"But—"

"Jalen," I interrupt again. "Have you ever told him?"

He holds my gaze for a second before looking away and shaking his head. "No," he says softly. "It would ruin everything."

He doesn't know that. In fact, I think the opposite might be true. Colby obviously worships the ground he walks on. But I think that might be a bit too much for him to hear right now.

"I don't know what's going on between the three of us," I say instead. "I'm sorry, this is very new and different. All I can tell you is that I mean it when I say that I care about you and Colby so much. I suggested this trip because I couldn't bear to be apart from you both over the holidays. And it's clear as day to me that you both are a little bundle of double trouble. I'm not really interested in doing anything with just one of you—unless maybe you wanted to go to a glitter factory, and Colby wanted to go read in a library."

Like I hoped, that gets a laugh out of him. He wipes his cheeks and takes a deep breath. "I have no idea what's going on, either," he admits with a little laugh. "But you're right. I do love spending time with you and my baby boy."

I nod. "So let's just keep doing that, okay? No more talk of getting in the way or anything. We're like...the Three Musketeers."

He crinkles his nose. "Who are they?"

I snort and drop my head against his neck. God, he smells so sweet. Before I can get carried away, I look back up and smile at him. "I'll tell you tomorrow. But for now...shall we agree that we're both going to look after Colby and I get to spoil you both equally. Deal?"

With a big inhale, he grins at me before snapping his fingers. "Deal, Daddy-O."

I let him go, but as I do, I swat his arse lightly. It takes us both by surprise, and he yelps as he jumps off the floor. "No more crying," I say firmly. "We've got a big day tomorrow. Go back to bed and have sweet dreams, okay?"

His eyes flick over my face for a second. "Yes, Daddy," he says softly.

He's vanished into the other room by the time I regain my senses.

Damn.

Being called 'Daddy' felt *exactly* as amazing as I hoped it would.

CHAPTER 11

Colby

I've never left the continent before.

The only reason I already have a passport was because I've flown over to Auckland a couple of times to visit my mum's sister. But it's really sinking in as I rub my fingers against the armrests of my seat that I'm actually going to Europe.

I can't decide if I'm terrified or ecstatic.

Taking a few deep breaths, I remind myself that it's going to be fine because Andreas is in charge, and he'll take care of everything. We're going back to his home country, so he'll know how to do everything. If I was traveling by myself, I'd be worried sick about using the wrong money or saying the wrong thing. But he'll make sure I don't do any of that.

Jalen asked if we could all wear our ugly Christmas jumpers for the flight, and Andreas enthusiastically agreed. He stressed several times to us how cold it can get on the plane, especially when you're trying to sleep, and how crappy the weather is going to be when we land in London.

In fact, he apologized several times in advance for how cold, wet, and especially *gray* it's going to be when we get there. I surprised myself by firmly reminding him that I'm so excited to be doing something so different and completely out of my comfort zone that the whole point is to have unusual weather. He chilled out after that.

The other thing he apologized for was 'only' being able to get us business class seats because first class were all sold out. But that still gave us access to the fancy lounge with all the free food and drink, and now that we're on the plane the seats are so big and comfy, and the staff are already being so nice to us—bringing us hot towels to freshen up our hands and faces as well as complimentary drinks before the plane has even taken off.

This is incredible. I feel so…special. The nice lady serving our area smiles at me every time she passes and calls me 'hun' whenever she gives me anything. Jalen is bouncing in his seat, and Andreas…

Well, he just keeps beaming at me and my best friend like he's won the lottery. I don't get it and I hate when the doubt starts creeping in. Because I know I'm nothing special. I'm pretty certain I'm not a bad person like my family tried to make me believe. Jalen has drilled that into me. But I'm not the kind of person who gets swept off their feet in crazy, romantic gestures.

No. I'm here because of Jalen, and that's more than fine. I wouldn't want to be sharing this experience with anyone else in the whole world.

"Are you okay?" Andreas asks, reaching between the partitions to slip his hand over mine.

We're in the middle set of three seats, but his is facing backward while mine and Jalen's are facing forward. It means we all have some privacy, but I can still see them if I try. Plus, apparently, there's a messaging system you can use between seats via the interactive screen in front of me, so if I really need to talk to Jalen privately, I can. Not that I feel like

I have things I want to keep from Andreas, but he'll probably fall asleep, and I can see Jalen being hyper and awake the entire time.

"I'm great," I answer truthfully. "This is like something out of a dream."

Andreas laughs and rubs his thumb against the back of my hand. It's such a small thing, but it feels enormous to me. He's just being nice, I'm sure. But it makes me feel so squirmy inside.

"You're probably not going to feel that way after seven hours, but I'm glad you're enjoying yourself now."

I frown, not quite remembering what he said before. "Is it only seven hours to London?"

"No, hun," he says kindly. "That'll take us to Singapore. When we get there, we'll all get off the plane for about an hour to stretch our legs while they refuel. Then it's another thirteen hours to Heathrow."

"And that's the London airport?"

"One of them," he says. "The biggest in London—actually —it's the biggest in all of Europe, if I remember correctly."

I bite my lip. "Oh," I say, immediately worrying about getting lost. But he shakes his head.

"We'll probably only see a bit of one terminal, so it won't seem so massive, I promise."

I let out a breath. "Okay, then. Sorry, I know I worry a lot."

He links our fingers together. I love it when he does that. "Worry as much as you need to," he says, which surprises me. Jalen is amazing, but he always just tells me not to worry, which I don't know how to do.

"Really?"

He chuckles. "It's natural to worry about unknown situations. Just promise me you'll always ask me any questions you have or run any concerns by me."

My skin feels hot under his hand. I try not to squirm in my seat. "I don't want to bother you," I mumble.

He tilts his head and gives me a patient look. "That's literally my job, Colby. I'm here to look after you and take care of you. It's my pleasure."

I inhale slowly and remind myself of the conversation I had with Jalen. Andreas is a Daddy. He might not specifically be *my* Daddy, but he is one, nonetheless. And it makes him feel good to be in charge and look after other people and pay for things. He's a gardener, and I'm a garden. I need to let him do some gardening.

"Thank you," I say softly.

His expression is filled with such warm affection I get lost in it. The moment stretches out until the intercom chimes overhead and the head flight attendant starts talking to us about safety protocols.

I do my best to listen, but it's difficult with Andreas's hand still on mine. That's far more interesting to focus on. But then he leans in to talk to Jalen, also taking his hand, and I wonder if I'm being selfish.

Should I let Andreas go so he can give all his attention to Jalen? That seems fair. I want them to be happy together. However, I'm not sure if I'm imagining it, but Andreas's grip on me seems to be just tight enough that I can't easily slip my hand away. So I decide to quit fretting over it and just let him hold on to us both.

We stay like that all throughout taxiing on the runway, the noisy takeoff, and into the sky. Once the seat belt signs go off, Andreas releases both of us and we begin the very long journey to the UK.

It's actually pretty fun. I thought it would be boring, and don't get me wrong, sometimes I find myself getting fidgety and frustrated. But the crew feed us a full meal as well as offer us snacks. There are so many films to watch, not to mention I've got a new romance book downloaded on my phone to read, and I even manage to get some sleep.

By the time we disembark in Singapore I do feel weird. There are a few shops we could go look at, but we focus on refilling our water bottles, and then Jalen makes me do a bunch of jumping jacks and stretches. I feel silly, and I know people are looking at us, but the movement really does help. Besides, all that matters is that Andreas joins in with us, so he obviously doesn't think we're being stupid.

For the second flight, I try and sleep as much as I can. Time has lost all meaning as we chase the sun around the sky. The crew feed us even more, and I put on an old Disney film that I know by heart. That helps me to doze off, and before I know it, we're starting our descent into Heathrow.

Nerves flare, and I'm not even sure why. It's really, very, completely too late to back out now as we touchdown on the tarmac. Not that I even want to. But the enormity of the situation is hitting me.

We're not just taking a trip with Andreas. We're meeting his family. At *Christmas*. What if they think it's weird that he's brought two friends with him? What if they don't like me? What if they don't like *Jalen*?

That gets my blood pumping. I might not be very good at defending myself, but hell will freeze over before anyone can be mean to my best friend.

But then I look over at Andreas as he reaches over to rescue my bag from the overhead bin, and I make myself remember that his family are not my family. He's excited about seeing them. They love him. They aren't ashamed of him and they're not trying to change who he is fundamentally as a person.

That gives me hope that they'll at least be polite to me and Jalen. They're being very kind by inviting us into their home for Christmas, after all.

I'm getting ahead of myself. First things first, we need to get off this plane and retrieve our luggage. I'm having high-key anxiety that my bag has gotten lost, and when Andreas notices me chewing on my thumbnail and asks what's wrong, for once, I simply tell him. Because he said I could.

Sure enough, he soothes my worries right away.

"That's very unlikely to happen," he assures me. "But if it does, we packed all your most precious things into your carry-on, remember? Worst-case scenario, we can buy you substitutes while we wait for your luggage to come back to you. But like I said, you'll probably be okay."

Some of the tightness eases from around my chest, and I thank him. But I don't fully breathe easy until I see it come through on the conveyor belt and it's back in my hands.

Once we've all got our suitcases, Andreas leads us over to signs pointing toward the underground. "Oh, I-I thought we'd get a taxi," I splutter. When I go into Sydney, I always study the metro map obsessively so I know exactly where I'm going. It didn't even occur to me to look up the London system, as Andreas is a big fan of taxis back home.

But he grins and shakes his head at me. "Nah. Traffic'll be a nightmare. I thought we'd take the Piccadilly Line into central, hop off at Piccadilly Circus, then walk up to see Carnaby Street. There are always amazing Christmas lights there, and the shops are really cool. We can grab some brunch, then after that, take the Vicky line from Oxford Circus down to Victoria Station. That's where we'll catch the train down to Brighton."

"That sounds awesome," Jalen says.

I can't help but giggle at how he slurs his words. As predicted, he got hyper on the plane and hardly slept the entire journey. Now he's dead on his feet, and Andreas has to keep steering him out of the way of people walking toward us.

"It does sound exciting," I say. "Will we be all right with our suitcases?"

Andreas shrugs. "It's London. It's packed no matter what. Do you think you'll be all right with yours for just a morning?" I nod eagerly, not wanting to spoil his fun plan. The way he smiles and says "Good boy" does very strange things to my insides indeed.

The tube is packed, and I'm glad Andreas buys us the correct tickets. There are escalators so it's not so bad with our luggage, but also elevators, which helps even more. We spend about half an hour on the underground, and Jalen and I struggle to stay awake the whole time.

Soon enough, though, we're ascending into the city above, and...Andreas was right. It's very gray, cold, and wet. But also so *alive*. Everyone and everything is moving so fast, and there's a kind of electricity in the air. It takes my breath away.

Carnaby Street is anything but gray. In fact, the gloomy weather means that we can still appreciate the lights, even though it's daytime. Andreas says the designs change every year, but this time, the neon lights have been shaped to create a miniature universe with planets, asteroids, and shooting stars. Andreas tells us that in the past, there have been rainbows, an underwater scene, mirror balls, butterflies—all sorts.

I like the space scene. It feels appropriate, considering how we all met. Sort of like kismet.

After finding a place to serve us massive traditional English breakfasts, we navigate the tube again to go to one of the city's overground train stations where Andreas buys the right tickets for us again.

"Fifteen minutes," he says in satisfaction, looking at the board to see when the next train is going to depart. "Perfect. Let's grab some tea, and then we can get ourselves settled."

"Coffee!" Jalen squeaks. "Coffee, please, coffee!"

Andreas laughs and rubs his back. "Coffee it is, hun."

Several minutes later, we have our hot drinks in takeaway cups and have been able to load our suitcases into the luggage racks at the end of the carriage. Our smaller bags have been placed overhead on a clear shelf by Andreas, and we managed to find four seats around a table so we can all see each other for the duration of the trip. I snuggle up next to a vibrating Jalen, and Andreas sits opposite. It's a bit like when he came to our flat to ask us on this trip with us. Jalen said later it felt like we were interviewing him for a job.

It's funny to think of our little flat still sitting there back there in Mount Druitt when we're all the way over here in London.

"So what time is your family expecting us?" I ask Andreas.

"Oh," he says, looking up from his phone with a nervous laugh. "They're not."

I blink. "They're…not?"

He shakes his head. "It's a surprise."

He can say that again.

CHAPTER 12

Jalen

I MIGHT BE HALLUCINATING FROM BOTH A LACK OF SLEEP AND caffeine overload, but I swear that Andreas just said that his family doesn't know we're on our way to visit.

"Come again?" I say, blinking rapidly and leaning over the table that separates me and Colby from Andreas. He's facing backward again like he did on the plane. I realize this because the train gives a jolt, then slowly starts moving out of the station.

"They don't know Jalen and I are coming?" Colby asks. "Or they don't know *any* of us are on the way?"

Andreas looks sheepish. It's not a particularly 'Daddy' expression, I must admit.

"Um…they don't have a clue that any of us are about to show up on the doorstep. I thought it would be fun!"

I narrow my eyes at him, calling bullshit. "Girl, are you serious? You don't think your mama will want to know? Moms have rules for these things. She'll want to get extra food and clean the sheets and other mom stuff."

"One," Andreas says, holding up a finger with a grin. "My mum might be a rubbish cook, but she's an *excellent* host, and she'll have bought enough food to feed the whole street. No kidding. Two, we're not staying with them. I found us a last-minute cancellation on an amazing holiday rental a short drive away, so we can have our own space and not be completely overwhelmed by the madness that is my family getting together."

I glance at Colby, still feeling a little unsure. "But why not tell them?" Colby asks.

"Are you ashamed of us?" I ask, as usual not willing to dance around the issue.

Andreas looks like he's been slapped. "Ashamed? What?"

He thrusts out his hands toward us, palms up, his eyebrows raised until Colby and I slip our hands against his. He takes a deep breath and visibly relaxes as he holds on to us.

"Thank you. Right, no. Absolutely not. If I'm being honest, I didn't mention it to my family so it wouldn't put any pressure on you guys to say yes. I know that this is a *massive* step forward in our relationship, and I was doing my best to keep it as low stakes as possible."

"Oh," I say with a chuckle. Of course he was protecting us. *Duh.*

"My family won't be put out," he says with a smile. "In fact, they are going to lose their *shit* in the best kinds of ways. There will be screaming and crying and hugging. And if I'm honest, if we spring this on them, they won't have had the time to overthink who you guys are or what's going on between us. We'll just tell them that you're my new friends because that's the truth."

I glance at Colby, who nods sweetly. I've been thinking nonstop about the conversation Andreas and I had the night before we left Australia. It's obvious none of us is feeling confident enough to name what's going on here because it's all so unfamiliar and uncertain.

But I believed Andreas when he said that he cares for both me and Colby equally, and he keeps proving to me how true that is. At least, it's feeling that way to me. Like right now. He's holding both our hands and rubbing against our knuckles with his thumbs, looking between us as he speaks.

However, I also meant what I said when I told him I was terrified about anything changing too much between me and Colby. He's the best friend I've ever had, and we all know how much sex complicates things. But I've been sharing a bed with him more and more these days, and I'd be lying if I said it wasn't getting that much harder to keep my hands to myself.

This relationship and the situation between us all is fragile, so I can actually sympathize with Andreas for wanting to keep it all on the downlow. If his family is as rambunctious as he's been telling us, they might have descended like vultures, picking us clean with all their questions.

Girl, I am *far* too pretty to be eaten alive.

I squeeze his hand. "It *is* the truth. We're all friends. *Best* friends!" I cry, bumping shoulders with Colby and making him laugh. "If you say they'll enjoy the surprise, then let's give them a good one."

Andreas smiles, looking relieved. "Okay, great. So what do you want to do when we arrive?" he asks. "Head straight over to my parents' place? Or check into the holiday rental first?"

I stare at him as I feel my very atoms vibrating in distress. "Boo, there's a surprise and then there's a downright horror show. You want us to go see your family after thirty hours of traveling?"

He glances at Colby, who shrugs. "Uh, it probably makes sense to drop our bags first and brush our teeth."

"Sugar!" I shriek with a snap of my fingers. "She needs an

entire spa day and a wardrobe change, not to mention some form of cat nap."

Andreas blinks and raises his eyebrows. "Okay. Understood," he says evenly and respectfully. "This evening it is."

Good. I would hate to have to spank my Daddy. I don't think we're quite there in the relationship.

Yet.

———

It takes about an hour for us to get down to Brighton, or so I'm told. I wouldn't know. Apparently, once we finished our conversation, I immediately fell dead asleep.

Luckily, our stop is the end of the line, so it doesn't matter that it takes Andreas and Colby a while to get me conscious again. But eventually, we manage to get ourselves and all our luggage off the train and onto the platform without anyone getting injured. I'm feeling extremely delicate from my lack of sleep, but Colby squeezes me to his side, giving me strength.

I grin down at him, not wanting to spoil any part of our adventure by being a grumpy kitty. I take a deep breath of fresh, cold air and shake myself before grabbing the handle of my suitcase.

"Lead the way, sir!" I cry at Andreas, giving him an elaborate wave of my hand. He laughs and snatches it out of the air to give my fingers a quick kiss before letting me go.

My heart skips a beat. I do that to Colby all the time, but he's only just started doing it back to me. That is the first time Andreas has done anything similar.

I like it. A lot. I hope that's okay.

We make our way down the platform, through the barriers, and across the concourse until we eventually find ourselves outside. It's not really raining, but it is very windy.

The sky is brighter here, though, than in London. Andreas points in front of us along the main street that the station sits at the end of.

"Down there is the beach," he says.

I love how Colby gasps. He's always lived by the water. I visited the beach a lot back home growing up, but it's like a compass to him. He navigates his life by the ocean, always knowing what direction it is in relation to everything else. I feel like it's almost…spiritual for him. More of a religion than the one his family tried to force onto him. I know being inland is one of the many things he dislikes about our place in Mount Druitt, and overlooking the bay is one of the things he loves the most about Andreas's apartment.

"Can we go down there?" he asks.

"Later," Andreas promises. "Right now, I think it's best if we head over to the holiday rental."

As much as I don't want to disappoint Colby, I have to agree with Andreas. It's been a LONG journey, mama, and this queen is ready for a shower, a metric ton of moisturizer, and some more shut-eye.

There's a taxi stand outside the station, so we wait our turn for one. We manage to get all our luggage in the trunk and pile our carry-on bags between me and Colby. Andreas sits up front and makes small talk with the driver. Between the little cases and backpacks, Colby and I hold hands. We don't say anything, but I can feel the excitement between us like electricity.

Colby starts sitting up straighter. The directions on the driver's phone say we're only a minute out, and there's something about the vista that's even prickling at my mind. It's so empty behind these houses. No trees or telephone poles.

I think we might be near the coast.

When the car comes to a halt, Colby bolts out the door and dances on his tiptoes by the trunk, his fists balled in an attempt to contain himself. I laugh as I grab the smaller bags and pull them out onto the curb while Andreas pays the driver and thanks him.

The house we're parked in front of is a two-story with a sloped roof and a light wooden fence running around the property. It looks like a modern build with big windows. Andreas said he managed to book it thanks to a last-minute cancellation.

I have a feeling we've really lucked out.

The taxi drives off as we drag our cases up the short pathway through the front yard that consists of a nicely kept lawn and an artsy little metal windmill collection. Andreas stops at the front door and gets out his phone. There's a small black box mounted on the wall that he punches a code into, then pulls the front down to reveal a key.

"Sorted," he says with a nod, clearly relieved that the key was where he was told it would be. He lets us inside, then barks out a laugh as Colby and I both abandon our cases in excitement to run inside.

"We'll come help in a second!" I promise as we rush through a sleek open-plan living room and kitchen. Colby is making a beeline for the French doors that lead out onto a large gray deck where I can see a black patio set of a table and chairs.

As Colby gets the door open and sprints out, I slow to a halt.

"There's a hot tub!" I scream in excitement. Although I'm sure Andreas was already aware of this fact when he booked it, and Colby hasn't stopped running.

I think it's amazing, anyway.

There's a short set of steps that leads down to a path that runs along the left of another neatly kept lawn. Hedges run either side of the back yard as well as the end of it, but the path finishes at a cute wooden gate. It's slatted so we can see through it.

I jog after Colby, who stops when he gets to it, reaching up to shove his fingers into his sandy blond hair. Then he wails.

"Look, Jay!" he yells back at me tearfully. I have to admit that I gasp as well as I reach the end of the yard.

The gate opens out directly onto the pebble beach.

We're literally by the sea.

I cover my mouth as I arrive by my best friend's side. It's a breathtaking view, and it's all ours. The gate is high, and there's a padlock on it for security reasons, but even between the slats, it's still spectacular.

"Do you like it?"

I whip around to find Andreas right behind us. Apparently, he's not mad that we left him with all the bags. He's grinning from ear to ear, his hands on his hips. He knows how good a job he's done here.

Colby and I throw ourselves at him, and we all find ourselves tangled in a fierce three-way hug.

"I love it," Colby sobs against Andreas's chest. I rub his back, knowing how tired I am and thinking he's probably not far off the same. "Thank you, Andreas. Thank you!"

To an outsider, it might seem strange that Colby is so emotional. But I think I understand exactly what's happening.

He can never go home. It was never really his home anyway, not in any of the ways that mattered. But being this close to the coast—even if it's the English Channel instead of the Pacific Ocean—might feel like a homecoming to him. Except this time, he's with someone who loves him—meeee—and someone who cares enough about him to give him this gift.

I think that's a kind of love.

I look up at Andreas, my heart full. I am definitely a BIG fan of this holiday home. But if I'm being honest, it's seeing how moved Colby is by Andreas's thoughtfulness and generosity that really makes me tearful. I bury my face against Andreas's neck for a moment, taking it all in.

He did this just for us. He really is amazing. But that uncertainty is still writhing in my stomach. He said that he cares for me and Colby equally, but what does that mean?

Because I want everything. I don't just want his time and attention. I want more of his touch. I want all he can give us and more for as long as he can. I want to share it with my best friend.

But I don't know if that's even going to be possible.

I'm uncertain how to convey so many thoughts, so I say the only thing that makes sense. Quietly. I'm not sure if Colby hears me or not, but soon enough, I hope I can say these words loudly and freely.

"Thank you, Daddy," I whisper into Andreas's ear.

CHAPTER 13

Andreas

I WAS AWARE WHEN I MANAGED TO NAB THIS HOLIDAY RENTAL at the last minute that I was incredibly jammy. Even if I'd have booked it months in advance, I still would have considered myself lucky to find something that was close to my parents' house, newly refurbished, spacious, with a hot tub, and not just a sea view but a garden path that leads directly to the beach.

Normally, I wouldn't say I'm a particularly superstitious person. But when this listing popped up in my search, I couldn't help but feel it was a sign from the universe.

I know it was a last-minute cancellation because the owners told me so. They had offered it at quite a reduced price in the hope that they wouldn't lose everything they should have made from the people who had to drop out after a medical emergency. When I insisted on paying the usual price, I could feel their relief coming through their emails.

Somewhere along the way, I think I picked up that Colby, in particular, liked the sea. Not from anything specific I can remember, so it must have just been a comment or two in passing. Therefore, I wasn't prepared for how emotional he got when he realized we'd be staying right on the coast. The poor little thing is practically sobbing against me.

Jalen is also hugging me, and I manage to catch his gaze and raise my eyebrows, silently asking him if he knows what this is about.

He rubs my back and mouths, "It's okay," with a nod. Maybe he'll be able to explain it to me later.

For now, I'm just massively happy that I got it so right. The whole point of this trip was to spoil the boys as much as possible. The fact that they love our home away from home means the world to me.

Almost as much as it meant to hear Jalen call me 'Daddy' again. It's like my heart has been given a warm hug and dipped in hot chocolate. I wonder if Colby would ever want to call me that. We keep dancing around the whole sugar Daddy business. It's been easier to acknowledge the sugar part of it. I think he's okay with me buying him things now.

But goddamn it, I would like to try Daddying him some more. He feels so good in my arms right now.

Eventually, though, I have to let him go. He withdraws with a shaky laugh, rubbing tears away from his face. "Sorry," he says sheepishly. "I blame the jet lag. But this place really is gorgeous."

"You've got nothing to apologize for," I assure him with a warm smile. "Why don't we go check out the inside of the house and find our rooms."

"Are Colby and I sharing again?" Jalen asks as he skips up the path. I chuckle as Colby and I follow behind him. Even sleep deprived, he's still such a joy.

"You can, if you like," I tell them both. "There are three rooms. The master, another double, and a twin. So you can choose to have your own, share with the two singles, or share with a double."

Or share with me.

The thought dangles tantalizingly in my mind, but of course I don't vocalize it. Like I said to Jalen, none of us really know where this relationship is going, and I certainly don't want to rush anything. It's enough that they're here at all.

I am curious about what room configuration they'll pick, though.

"I'm happy to keep sharing," Jalen says with a shrug as he twirls around in front of us, briefly facing us and giving a nonchalant smile. I have a hunch, though, that he feels anything but casual about Colby's response.

"Umm," Colby says. His cheeks are pink, but that could just be from the wind. "Yeah, that's been fun, actually. It makes it feel more like a holiday. You know, like it's a sleep-over or something."

"Nice," Jalen says, still trying to play it cool. How I could have ever thought he wasn't madly in love with his best friend, I'll never know. "Let's stick with the double bed, then. I think I'd fall out of a twin after so many years."

They both laugh, but I don't miss that Colby also glances at me when Jalen's back is turned. He looks as if he's asking for permission, so I nod subtly. That seems to be enough for him.

"Yeah, totally," he agrees with Jalen.

I wonder if he even realized he just did that. Defer to me, I mean. Bloody hell. I'm already Daddying him in so many ways. Considering I've never done this before, I sure seem to feel like I know a lot about it, and I definitely want to get a move on with actually putting it into practice.

It's a relief to get back inside, where the heating is on, and the aggressive sea breeze can't get to us anymore. I'd previously managed to haul all the bags into the entrance hall at least, so we all grab our own and make our way upstairs to find the bedrooms. Mine is the biggest with an en suite, but the other double room has the best view of the beach, and my heart swells, feeling like the universe is talking to us again. It's like they were meant to share that room.

We busy ourselves taking showers and getting unpacked. After such a long trip, it's blissful to get clean and put on fresh clothes. Jalen wants to nap, and Colby says he's got something he needs to do on his busted old laptop, so I decide to go find the local shop and get us some basics in, like tea, coffee, milk, and cereal.

As I walk down to the mini supermarket, I daydream about buying them both fancy new laptops. I really don't want to overwhelm them, but in my imagination, we've been friends for ages, and they let me do stuff like that for them without it feeling like an enormous gesture. As my fantasy wanders along, I think about how maybe that could be next year's Christmas presents.

When I return, they're both still upstairs, so I put the few bits of shopping away, make myself a cup of tea, then take a stroll down to the beach. Even someone like me—for whom money is no object—can't help but be blown away by how special it is to just wander down the garden and see the English Channel. The waves crash against the shore in a soothing rhythm, which is a good thing, because I'm starting to get nervous.

Deep down I knew it was pretty crazy to come all this way and not warn my family. But I've been getting continuous updates from the group chat so I know that my sister and the girls are already at my parents' house, as planned, and extended family will be joining them on Christmas Day.

Logically, I'm sure they'll be beyond thrilled to see me. Our family has a history of surprising one another with relatives from overseas. My only hesitation is how they're going to receive Jalen and Colby.

As much as I wanted to bring them on a trip of a lifetime,

I'm also aware that some people might be confused by what's going on and have questions. They're younger than me and there are two of them. My relatives can interrogate me all they like. I'd just hate for anyone to make my boys feel uncomfortable, though.

I take a long breath in, filling my lungs with cold sea air. Who do I really think is going to be a dick? Anisha's ex, Gregory, won't be there. He was the only one who ever tried to be passive-aggressively homophobic with me, but it never got him anywhere.

I might have the odd aunt or uncle who will put their foot in it, but hopefully people will simply accept that I've brought some friends home from Sydney and that's it. If anyone asks how we all know each other, I've already encouraged the boys to tell the Jurassic Galaxy origin story. That's what brought Jalen and Colby together as well, after all. And if anyone points out that we only just met, I've decided my answer will be "So?"

This is ridiculous. I'm completely overthinking it all. My parents freaked out about my sexuality in a completely different time. There wasn't a fraction of the representation that there is these days, and I've talked to them a great deal about the advancements in treating HIV. They know it's perfectly treatable, and in fact there is a strong possibility it could be completely eradicated by the end of the decade.

But there's a part of me that's still that teenage boy, feeling the sting and horror of true rejection by the people who I thought would always love me unconditionally. It doesn't matter that now I know they were just afraid for their son. A part of me is scared they'll do it again.

A bigger part of me is terrified they'll reject Jalen and Colby.

Especially Colby. He's already lost his own terrible family. I couldn't stand it if mine hurt him as well.

I wander back up to the house with my empty tea mug, toying with the idea of at least messaging my sister. However, I'm distracted when one of the upstairs windows flings open and Jalen leans out of it.

"THERE you are!" he shrieks. "We have an emergency!"

I bolt the rest of the way up the garden and into the house, expecting it to be on fire. When I don't see any smoke, I take the steps two at a time to reach their bedroom.

Which is also not on fire. But it certainly is covered in a lot of clothes.

"An-*dre*-as, help!" Jalen whines, stamping his foot and holding up a bundle of several different scraps of fabric at me. I assume they are all tops. Or skirts. Maybe scarves?

I let out a breath and arch an eyebrow at him. "This is the emergency?"

"We don't know what kind of occasion it's going to be tonight. Party? Casual? Formal?" He bats his eyelashes at me. "We have to be *fabulous*, darling!"

I wave my hands at him. "Okay, okay," I say, understanding that this actually would be pretty stressful for him. Colby is just looking at him with wide eyes like he's questioning why he even got on a plane in the first place. "I'd go with party," I say. "My family like a bit of pizzazz, and I know my nieces love any excuse to get their glitter and sequins out."

Jalen visibly sags in relief. "What a *sensible* family you have," he says with a completely straight face. "That narrows down the options by about half. Thank you."

As Jalen rummages through what appears to be most of his wardrobe, Colby turns to me and anxiously plucks at his knitted jumper. It's baggy, but in a way that looks like it's on purpose. He's paired it with light blue jeans, and with his freshly washed hair the whole look is so adorably soft that I want to hug him to me and never, ever let go.

"Do *I* look okay?" he whispers. Jalen has some perky pop music playing, so he doesn't seem to hear Colby's question, but I certainly do.

"You look perfect," I tell him truthfully. How could I ever worry about my family not liking these boys? They're both so sweet in their own very different ways.

Eventually, Jalen is ready to go in a chic, frilly black-and-white shirt, shimmery purple trousers, and the same heeled boots he wore to that first dinner we all had together. He gets a bit sulky when I make him put a coat on, but after we step outside in the dark to get into the Uber, I hear a sharp gasp and he doesn't say another word about it.

Score one for Daddy.

When we're in the car and on our way, I'm surprised that Colby slips his hand over my shoulder. I turn and look at him in the back seat. "Are you all right?" he asks so genuinely it makes my heart ache. "You said it's been a long time since you saw your parents."

I nod. I've video called with them a *lot.* But that's not the same as seeing and hearing them in person. Definitely nothing compared to getting hugs from them both.

"I'm good," I tell him, ignoring the little fluttering of nerves that I can't quite explain or banish. Hopefully they'll go away on their own once we arrive.

The house is just how I remember it. They moved down here when I was in my late twenties—largely because I helped them with the deposit—so I've never lived here myself. But I have a lot of fond memories of family get togethers, and some of the nerves mercifully turn to excitement.

It's a large two-story detached house with a relatively long front drive and a pebble garden running alongside it with numerous potted plants. White lights adorn the base of the roof, the windows, and around the front door in an incredibly tasteful display that looks like snow has really fallen. I remember when they used to put a sign out front that said "Santa, stop here!" for the girls, but they're too old for that now.

I can't help but think that my boys might enjoy something like that, though.

I'm pulled from such a silly thought by the Uber stopping outside the front door. As the boys spill out of the car, I thank the driver and give him a five-star rating as well as a tip. Then it's my turn to get back out into the cold.

And suddenly, I'm standing in front of the door, knowing that I have to be the one to ring the bell.

In the end, I push down my nerves and do it for my boys. I have to be strong for them. I don't want them to think there's anything to be nervous about. I brought them all this way after all. So I step up and push the button.

There are raised voices from within. Probably people yelling that someone needs to get that and others asking who it could be.

I'm so glad it's my sister who opens the door.

For a second, Anisha just stares at me, her jaw dropping and her eyes growing wide. Then she screams so loudly I fear it'll disturb the houses three doors down, but selfishly, I don't care.

"OhmygodohmygodohmyGOD!" she shrieks as she throws her arms around me and almost knocks me off my feet. "Guys, come look! LOOK!"

The first to come into the hall are her daughters—Isla, twelve, and Esme, sixteen. If possible, they scream even louder than their mum as they launch themselves at me as well. Then it's my dad, who clutches his chest, and my mum, who just starts crying. That gets a lump in my throat as they crowd around me in a massive cuddle pile, all talking at once about how terrible I am, asking each other if they knew, and telling me how good I look.

When the need to breathe becomes a bit too much, I gently push them off me, grinning with tears in my eyes. "Uh, everyone. I'd like to introduce you to my friends, Jalen and Colby. They've come all the way from Australia to spend the holidays with me. Well, with us."

"Hello, hello!" my mum coos, ushering us in with her hands. "It's freezing out there, come on in! It's a pleasure to meet you both."

She immediately begins to fuss over them both, but Anisha pulls sharply on my arm to extract me slightly from the excitable group. I blink at her as she narrows her eyes at me. "Are these the dinosaur beach friends?" she demands in a low voice.

I take a breath before smiling at her. "Yes," I say confidently and firmly.

There's a beat until her face splits into a devilish grin. "They're *cute*, baby bro. Are they yours?"

I consider her question as I look over at them being hugged aggressively by our mother.

"I certainly hope they might be," I murmur.

CHAPTER 14

Colby

"THANK YOU, MRS. LAU," I SAY AS ANDREAS'S MUM TAKES MY coat from me.

She blows a raspberry and waves her hand. "Call me Tianna. We're all family here. When did you boys arrive?"

"This morning," I answer.

"Do you mean we posted your presents all that way for nothing?" Andreas's sister grumbles at him.

He laughs sheepishly. "If it helps, I brought them all back with me to open on here Christmas Day."

"That doesn't really pay for the postage, now does it?" Anisha counters with a raised eyebrow.

Andreas grins at her. "Would a case of red wine make up for it?"

Anisha throws open her arms. "Merry Christmas!"

Tianna puffs her cheeks out and shakes her head. "You must be shattered," she says to me and Jalen. "Come on. You come sit down and let me fuss over you. Your timing was spot on. We were just about to have dinner."

We're interrupted as Jalen removes his coat as well, and

Andreas's two nieces both gasp. "You look lush," the younger one says.

"You look like you should be performing on Strictly," the older one agrees before sticking her hand out. "I'm Esme. Pronouns she/her."

"I'm Isla!" the younger one adds, jostling her sister for Jalen's attention and also shoving her hand forward. "My pronouns are she/her, too!"

Andreas was right about their outfits. They both have sparkly tops on over black leggings and glitter around their eyes. Esme has bright red hair extensions woven into her braids, and Isla has a cute bow nestled in her big natural curls.

"Kids these days," Andreas's dad says with a chuckle, presumably referring to how they naturally included their pronouns in their introductions. His tone is fond, though, not mocking like my own father's would have been.

"I think it's really cool," Andreas says.

"That's because I'm a really cool mum," his sister says with a grin.

"Aren't you both adorable," Jalen says, touching one hand to his chest and using the other to shake with the girls. "And so polite. I'm Jalen and you can totally use he/she/they for me. It's all love. And this is my best friend in the whole wide world, Colby. He uses he/him."

"Hi," I say shyly.

"So you're Australian," Isla says to me before looking at Jalen. "But you're American?"

Jalen nods, slipping his arm through mine and following Tianna into the living room. "Yep. We've been besties for years online. Then I moved to Sydney this summer."

This *winter,* I correct mentally, but I guess for everyone else here it would have been the summer. That's weird.

As we enter the room, my attention is immediately drawn

to an enormous pile of floof lying on a rug by the lit fire-place. The bottom half is gray, and the top is white with a pink bow tied at the end. As we enter, the mop moves to reveal a pair of black eyes, a black nose, and a pink tongue that lols out as the lump begins to pant. A gray tail with a white tip emerges and slowly starts to wag.

"Puppy!" Jalen shrieks, rushing over to the dog. I just stand still for a second, desperately trying not to let the tears fall that have gathered in my eyes. I adore dogs, but obvi-ously I was never allowed to have one. My mother said they were disgusting and smelly.

Andreas's own mother pipes up from behind us. "Actually, she's more of a grandma than a puppy, but don't tell her that."

Andreas puts his hand on my lower back to get my atten-tion as he smiles down at me. "Do you want to come say hello?"

"Yes, please," I say breathlessly. We go over to the gentle giant, sitting on the carpet to stroke her. The bow is keeping her hair out of her face so she can see. "What's her name?"

"River," Andreas says fondly. "River Song. Mum's always been a massive Doctor Who fan, and now we all are, so we've also had Sarah-Jane, Barbara, Ace, and Rose."

"Hello, River!" Jalen coos as we all pet her. She looks between us, basking in all the attention.

"Ahh, I missed so much time with her," Andreas says sadly.

His sister squeezes his shoulder. "You're here now. That's what counts."

"We should probably let her sleep," Andreas says as he gets to his feet. I don't really want to move, but I want to do what's best for River. "We can come say hello again later when things calm down," Andreas says.

"So you met Uncle Andy in Sydney?" Esme asks from one of the sofas where everyone else has taken their seats.

Jalen drags me away from the drowsy dog onto a sofa, sandwiching me between him and Andreas. Oh, *god.* He's pressed up against me, and immediately I struggle to think about anything else. I'm used to my best friend manhandling me, but Andreas is off-limits. I promised myself. But he just smiles at me and puts his arm around my back, and *holy crap* I really can't think straight.

He and Jalen are telling the story about how we all met through our love of Jurassic Galaxy, which the girls both look up on their phones as apparently they've never heard of it. Jalen launches into his usual speech about how great it is and why, while Andreas's parents start bringing in plates of party food and fixing people with drinks. I politely accept some kind of flavored sparkling water, whereas Jalen jumps at the offer of prosecco, and Andreas gets a beer.

I can feel both Andreas's parents looking at us with interest, especially his mum. But I'm pretty attuned to when there's an actual problem or simmering hostility thanks to my upbringing. I can't say I feel that from them now. Just curiosity.

"You really should have told us you were coming," Andreas's dad—Yuen—gently chides as he and Tianna also sit down. People start helping themselves to food, but I'm too shy. "We could have met you at the airport."

Andreas shakes his head. "That's so kind of you, Dad. But it was such a last-minute decision and we wanted to surprise you."

"You wanted to make your own mother cry, you mean," his mum scoffs, but she hasn't stopped smiling since we arrived. "You always did like a bit of drama. And you," she says, looking between me and Jalen. I try not to wince as my heart picks up speed, bracing myself for what's to come. "Thank you, both."

Well, I really wasn't expecting that.

"Um, you're welcome?" I say, completely unsure.

"For what?" Jalen asks, ever the blunt one.

Andreas's parents laugh and share a look. "For coming all this way with Andreas," Tianna says warmly. "You must be very good friends to do that."

I feel myself blushing, and I'm not sure what to say. Jalen comes to my rescue, as usual. "Andreas is very easy to be friends with," he cries, patting Andreas's head over mine and making him laugh. "He's so kind and fun to be around. Wait until we tell you about our awesome vacation rental!"

Tianna tuts. "You could have stayed here," she grumbles.

Andreas flicks his eyebrows at her. "But this place is literally on the beach," he says with a grin. "With a hot tub."

"Can we come visit?" Isla pipes up.

Esme smacks her knee, and I freeze in panic. "Don't be rude," Esme says to her younger sister.

Isla sticks her bottom lip out. "Mum!" she protests. She doesn't seem to care that she's just been struck at all. In fairness, it was only a light tap, but still my heart is racing.

Anisha rolls her eyes and sips her red wine. "Both of you, behave. Isla, it's a holiday home, they might not want visitors. Esme, don't hit your sister."

They both mumble apologies but soon forget about the spat as they load their plates up with the fancy looking savory pastries that Yuen just bought in, straight from the oven. I take a few breaths and calm down.

This isn't my family.

I've never been around a group of people that got on so easily before. It's intimidating. I'm so afraid of saying the wrong thing or embarrassing myself. They're just so rambunctious, but there doesn't feel like there's any tension underlying anything they say or do. My mother would have been offended ten times over already from the little jabs and people laughing at each other.

I was sort of aware that Andreas had leaned forward to get some food from the coffee table, but he gets my full attention when he slides a plate in front of my nose. I look at him and frown in confusion.

"For you," he explains quietly as people talk all around us.

I bite my lip and see that Jalen is currently helping himself. "What about you?"

"I'll get mine next," Andreas says warmly. "Is there anything else you fancied? I tried to get you a bit of everything, as I wasn't sure if you could reach the table from there."

My insides melt a little. I can reach just fine. He just saw that I was fretting and took matters into his own hands.

Jalen's right. He's a natural Daddy. I feel honored that he's giving me that kind of attention. I know I promised to push him toward Jalen, but I can't help but savor this moment for just a little while.

"Thank you," I say sincerely. "That's so sweet of you."

I realize Jalen is watching us. When our eyes meet, Jalen beams at me like he's pleased or proud. But I feel guilty. I don't want to take Andreas away from him.

"You weren't wrong," Jalen says to Andreas, breaking the moment. "Your mom made a ton of food."

"Always better to have too much than not enough," Tianna says, wagging her finger. "And it's all stuff you just bung in the oven. Even I can't muck that up."

"I don't know about that," Anisha says with a raised eyebrow, then ducks as her mother makes a show of pretending to clap her around the head.

This time, I flinch so badly I almost drop my plate.

Andreas is there in a flash, like a superhero. He grabs the edge before my food can fall on the carpet, saving me from having to die from extreme mortification. My heart is in my throat, though, and I struggle to take in decent breaths.

"Are you okay?" he murmurs. Luckily, no one else seems to have noticed my faux pas.

I swallow and manage to inhale properly, still feeling pretty stupid. Logically, I knew that his mum wasn't about to hit his sister. They were just playing. But my instincts kicked in before my brain could, and I freaked out.

"Yeah, thanks," I say shakily.

He doesn't ask me to explain myself. He just waits until I've got a firm hold on my plate again, then rubs my back in a soothing way. I could almost cry. How does he manage to make me feel so much better with just a couple of simple gestures?

I need to be brave and try to adapt to the new situation. This *isn't* my old house or the people I grew up with. It's an entirely new environment, so if I can manage it, I need to stop applying the old rules. Andreas is here to protect me, after all, so this is a safe place to try new things, if possible.

I think of my favorite Jurassic Galaxy character, Buckets. He was an orphan who took a long time to trust the rest of the crew. But when it really mattered, he did, and it saved all their lives.

Can I be like Buckets? It's appalling thinking of putting myself out there and being vulnerable with people who could hurt me. But if I don't start now, then when? Besides, there's no one who makes me feel bold like Andreas and Jalen do. They're by my side right now—literally pressed against me— and I do my best to feed off their courage.

Tentatively, I begin to nibble on some food. But it's not long before there's another commotion. "Andy? I hear Andy!" a new voice calls from out in the hallway. She sounds frail but excited.

"Nai Nai?" Andreas cries in disbelief.

"I thought you were sleeping, Mum," Yuen says as he gets to his feet. A little old lady with thick glasses and perfectly permed white hair shuffles into the living room with a walking stick. Yuen gently helps her to an armchair and drapes a crocheted blanket over her lap.

"You having fun without me!" she accuses, making everyone laugh. She has a strong accent but speaks English with confidence.

Andreas puts his plate on the coffee table before extracting himself from the couch to go over and give her a careful hug. "I didn't know you were here," he says thickly as she pats his back.

"I don't know *you* here!" she cries in response, swatting his shoulder and making him laugh. "You bad boy."

"It was a surprise, Nai Nai," he says warmly. "I'd like you to meet my friends, Jalen and Colby. They traveled all the way from Sydney with me. Guys, this is my grandmother, Zhen."

"It's lovely to meet you," I say earnestly.

"Hi, Zhen!" Jalen cries with a wave.

"Oh, you pretty," Zhen says, peering through her glasses at us. "Both of you. You my Andy's boyfriends?"

Tianna splutters and laughs. Yuen seems confused. The girls look at us in genuine interest. Anisha glances away and takes a large gulp of wine through her smirk. Andreas smiles indulgently at his grandma.

"We're good friends, Nai Nai. Can I get you some food?"

She squints at the table. "Anything spicy?" That gets a laugh from her family as they make her up a plate and fetch a chili dip to make it more to her liking.

My heart is still banging in my chest, and I'm worried my face has gone bright red with embarrassment. I can't believe she asked that, and although it got plenty of reactions, no one said it was disgusting or outrageous. In fact, they were either just surprised or intrigued.

But that's crazy, right? Threesomes are something people

do to be kinky. When couples want to revitalize their love life. None of us are dating. Yet this sweet lady from a far less open-minded generation just casually asked if Jalen and I were her grandson's boyfriends. She even sounded kind of hopeful.

I glance over at Jalen. He was listening in on the conversation that's going on about some other sci-fi TV show the family have been watching. But when he senses my gaze, he turns and smiles at me.

He doesn't seem put out at all by the insinuation.

Could…could that be a thing?

I've been beating myself up anytime Andreas doted on me because I was worried about getting in the way of him and Jalen. But he kept making everything so equal between us, it was hard not to feel like it was okay. Like I wasn't really taking up *too* much space. And I promised myself that if—when—things changed, I'd gracefully step aside.

But…what if I don't have to?

What if this plucky granny has cut through all the bullshit and hit the nail on the head?

Could Jalen and I keep sharing Andreas like we have done? But in a more intimate way?

The thought makes me feel shaky. Of course Andreas senses any little change in me, and rubs my back again. "You good?"

I blink at him, looking into his beautiful eyes, and my insides swoop. Am I insane? Would Andreas really be interested in me in that way? I didn't think it could be possible with Jalen right there next to me. But I can't think of a single time he's made me feel anything less than cherished. In fact, he goes out of his way to make sure we both get the same amount of time and attention from him.

He asked us to come with him to the other side of the world and meet his family, for heaven's sake.

It's really hard for me to believe that anyone would be interested in me. I look at Jalen again, my heart aching like it always does. I love him so much, and I know he doesn't feel the same way. But maybe…well, I've read online about open relationships and polyamory and stuff like that.

Perhaps Andreas really could be a sugar Daddy to both of us. I know he already is, sort of, but perhaps there could be some cuddles and kisses, too? How would Jalen feel about that? We'd still be close that way. I'd still have my best friend and maybe something more with Andreas as well.

I have no idea if I've lost my mind or if I'm seeing what's been in front of my eyes all this time. But there's a tiny flicker of hope that's lit in my chest, and I carefully guard it for the rest of the night.

Who knows? I'm sure stranger things have happened.

CHAPTER 15

Andreas

THANKS TO OUR JET LAG, WE DON'T LAST ALL THAT LONG AFTER Nai Nai's appearance at my parents' house. Knowing we have several days of socializing ahead of us, I don't mind so much as I order an Uber and bundle my boys back home.

It doesn't hurt that my heart is both somehow light and full.

Deep down, I didn't really think that my family would have a problem with me bringing my new friends home for Christmas. The reality of the evening is still extremely comforting. They loved them. Jalen was obviously dazzling, and my nieces adored him, but I could see the way my mum kept fussing over Colby as well, naturally seeking out the person in the room who needed just that little bit of extra care and attention. Everyone was genuinely friendly and engaging. Even old River got up to say goodbye to them, her tail wagging as she headbutted them both for attention.

And then there was Nai Nai. Good *lord*. Trust that it would be her to immediately call out the elephant in the room. My first reaction was of course to worry about how the boys would react to being called my boyfriends. Colby was understandably rattled. I'm sure the idea that anyone would want to date him is tragically a foreign concept to him. But Jalen barely seemed to be bothered at all. In fact, I think he preened.

As I lie in bed that night, desperately tired but my whirring brain keeping me awake for just a little longer, I can't help but feel like she's given me permission. I'm not sure how much I can keep lying to myself.

I want both of these boys. I want them to truly be mine. I want to hold them and kiss them and make them feel good in every way I can imagine. I want to provide for them and protect them the way a good Daddy should. I know for sure that Jalen feels that way about Colby and I'm almost certain about me as well. The only piece of the puzzle is how Colby feels about us two.

I have a strong suspicion there's attraction for both of us, but between them, he's the one I'm most concerned about getting it wrong. He's so delicate, and I'd hate to damage or break the wonderful relationship we've already built between the three of us.

But out of the two of them I know it's Colby that needs to be loved the most. Jalen is easy to adore. He invites it in with a warm embrace. Colby doesn't know *how* to be loved. He's been trained to flinch and run from people who are close to him. He's had his vulnerabilities used as weapons against him.

It's become my mission to prove to him that he's worthy of love. I know that Jalen and I can love the hell out of him if only he'd let us.

The next morning, I wait for the boys to rise naturally. From my experience so far, the jet lag this way around isn't so bad. When I moved to Sydney in the first place, I had several days of finding myself wide awake at three in the morning no matter what I did. But we all seem to naturally surface between eight and nine o'clock, moving through the bathrooms and getting dressed.

"What do you want to do today?" I ask them as the kettle boils for tea and coffee. I bought a couple of different types of cereal but also have bread to make toast as well as a bunch of bananas and some apples. We might have eaten a great deal last night, but a lot of it was coated in some kind of carb or dipped in cheese. I'll feel better knowing my boys have some nutrients in them to start the day. Especially as it's Christmas Eve, and I'm sure the next few days will consist of nothing but indulgence.

"Can we walk along the beach?" Colby asks hopefully.

I'm about to say yes when I have another idea. "Of course. But would you guys like to go down to the pier? That way we can be by the sea, but also there are different kinds of rides and food places."

"What?" Jalen asks. "A pier? Yes! What? Oh my god!"

"That sounds so fun," Colby says breathlessly. "I didn't realize there was a pier."

I nod. "Once upon a time, there were three piers, actually. The old one was more like a suspension bridge and that's almost all gone now. The West Pier used to be really popular last century, but it closed down in the seventies, I think. Then it burned down about twenty years ago. We can go look at the wreckage if you like."

Jalen wrinkles his nose. "Maybe. But the third pier is the fun one, right?"

I laugh and ruffle his curls, making him grin. "Yes, that's the one people generally mean when they talk about Brighton Pier. Do you boys like roller coasters? They have a few different kinds of rides and attractions."

"I've never been on one," Colby admits, looking worried.

I reach out and squeeze his hand. "No pressure," I assure

him. "We can go take a look, and if you don't fancy it, we don't have to do anything that makes you uncomfortable."

"Of course," Jalen agrees wholeheartedly. But then he looks back at me. "I can still go on them, though, right? You guys can go get cotton candy and watch me be awesome."

That makes us all laugh, and I promise them that we'll all have a fun day doing whatever we want. I told my parents that we'd come over for dinner again before spending the whole of Christmas Day with them, so we've got several hours to ourselves to explore Palace Pier.

I've been here several times, but there's something incredible about showing my guests around. Knowing my dad is making us a proper dinner tonight with several kinds of vegetables, I indulge the boys and let them have fish and chips for lunch. It would be rude not to while on the British seaside, after all.

In order to make sure our food is settled before going on any rides, we spend a little time walking up and down the extremely windy pebble beach. I'm glad I made both the boys bundle up, as the elements are strong along here. It's almost impossible to hold a proper conversation, but that doesn't really matter as Jalen and Colby run up and down like puppies. They throw stones into the water and take lots of selfies as they squeal in delight. Before we turn back to return to the pier, we simply stand with Colby and look at the water for a while, enjoying the crashing waves.

I decide to tackle the biggest ride to start with and see if Colby is feeling up to it. We wait in front of the Turbo roller coaster for a bit, sizing it up. "Okay," he says all of a sudden. "Let's do it."

"Are you sure?" I check.

He nods, his cheeks pink from the wind. "Yes. I don't want to regret not at least giving it a go."

I squeeze his shoulder, bursting with pride. "Good boy."

He beams at the praise, and Jalen throws his arms around him. "Yay! You can do it, boo-boo! It'll be fun!"

The line isn't too bad, thanks to the time of year and the weather. The carriages fit four people with two in the front and two in the back. As it's not busy, they don't bother trying to find a single rider to go with us.

"Who do you want next to you, Colby?" I ask. "I don't mind where I sit," I emphasize.

He nibbles his lip, and I'm conscious we only have seconds to make a decision. But he surprises me again by answering quickly. "Can I sit with Jalen? And then you can watch over us from behind."

"Perfect," I say with a grin.

My boys hold hands as the ride begins. It's incredibly tame compared to some of the roller coasters I've done in my time, but I think that makes it perfect for Colby's first one. The crank up isn't that long, and rather than dropping right away, it goes around for a semi-circle allowing us to look out over the water. When we finally drop, the boys lift up their hands and scream into the wind as the train thunders through the one and only loop, then the next several increasingly smaller drops. It's probably over in under a minute and a half, but when we disembark, both of them are grinning from ear to ear.

"Can we do it again?" Colby asks breathlessly.

How can I say no?

We ride the Turbo a couple more times, then the Crazy Mouse which is a smaller coaster with individual four-person pods that spin as they hurtle along the twisty track. We all feel a little queasy after that one, so we stop to get hot drinks and then venture into the shelter of the arcade for a while. We play some silly games, and the boys each win a stuffed animal to take home. I make sure to put the fluffy turtle and shark into my backpack for them.

To end the afternoon, I agree to go on the log flume. The idea of getting wet in December doesn't appeal to me much, but the boys are so excited about it I figure it won't be so bad if we head home right after. There's an option to buy ponchos that I insist on for the sake of the Uber's interior as well as an attempt to keep us reasonably dry.

It's totally worth it, though, as not only is it a fun little ride, but they snap a photo of you on the way down. My heart creeps into my throat as I look at the image they captured of us looking exhilarated. It's so authentic with no kinds of barriers up, especially from Colby. Just three people having a blast together. I don't hesitate to buy it as well as get a digital copy sent to me so we can all have versions of it when we get back home.

I know I'm going to want to remember this day forever.

Dinner with my family is lovely. I can't believe I wasn't going to come back to the UK for this. It's been so easy to fall into my solitary routine, but I'd be missing out on all these special moments. My dad has made a curry that people can adapt to make as creamy or as spicy as they want. My boys unabashedly put several dollops of yogurt in their bowls while Nai Nai cackles at the head of the table, sprinkling chili flakes on hers like hundreds and thousands.

Jalen is nonstop as he chatters away about our day, which isn't surprising. What does delight me is how Colby manages to butt in and tell a few stories of his own. Whenever he does, Jalen immediately shuts up and watches him like he hung the moon.

These boys are going to break my heart if they're not careful. I just want to bottle every moment up with them. I'm aware we're fast approaching a point of no return, and my only dilemma is whether I should do something about it while we're still on our trip or wait until we get back home. The thought of living together in the holiday rental and not making the most of it is slightly killing me. But on the other hand, what if it doesn't go the way I expect and then we're in an awkward situation for the rest of our time here?

I decide to just keep going with the flow but stay mindful of looking for opportunities. From our conversation back at my apartment, I'm certain that Jalen is waiting for me to make some kind of move. The deciding factor is Colby. It's him I'm watching intently to take my cue.

The best way to do that is to keep giving us chances to do special things together.

So we leave my parents' place at a reasonable time again, promising to be back bright and early for Christmas morning. However, I have a little plan for when we get back to the house, and I don't want jet lag to get the best of us again.

"How about," I say as we walk up to the front door, "we keep our coats and shoes on, I make us some hot chocolate, and we walk down to the beach?"

Colby gasps. "Really? Can we?"

I nod, and Jalen claps his gloved hands. "Christmas on the beach, UK style!"

"That's exactly what I thought," I admit with a chuckle.

It's only instant powder hot chocolate from the little supermarket, but I make it with whole milk, spray whipped cream on top, and add a couple of fluffy marshmallows to the bottom of each mug, so they'll be a gooey mess by the time we get to the end of our drinks. I also slip the surprise I bought from the shop into my coat pocket without either of them noticing.

It might be windy, but it's a clear night and the moon is bright, so we can see pretty well as we make our way down to the pebble beach. Our chocolate doesn't stay that hot for long, so we drink it reasonably quickly, eating what's left of the marshmallows in delight.

In my other pocket, I'd put a bottle of water which I now

use to fill up my empty mug. "Can't we wash that back in the house?" Colby asks in confusion when he sees what I'm doing.

I flash him a grin. "Oh, of course. I'm not washing it. That's for safety."

They both frown at me. "Safety for what?" Jalen asks.

That's when I pull the slim box of sparklers from my other pocket along with a lighter. "For these."

Jalen gasps. "Oh my god! I haven't played with sparklers since I was a kid!"

"I don't think I ever have," Colby says dubiously.

Jalen immediately takes his hand and kisses the back of it through his glove. "Don't worry! It's easy. And Andreas brought the water to put them out when we're done. They're pretty!"

I can see Colby continue to frown as we each get one out of the box, and I take on the responsibility of lighting them. Despite the wind, they crackle into life, illuminating my boys' faces. I think Colby was maybe wondering what the point of them was, but as soon as he's holding the sparking stick in his hand, I suspect he understands that the point is just pure joy and fun. Without even needing to be told, he starts waving his one around, creating shapes in the dark.

"Wee!" Jalen shrieks, making circles and figures of eight. My heart aches to see them so happy.

This day really has been magical. Once the first round die out, we put the hot ends into the mug of water. Then I light another pair for the boys to play with some more. Rather than get one for myself, I pull my phone out and start taking pictures. I've captured so many beautiful moments today. My phone is usually pretty devoid of any photos, but I'm going to have a whole album's worth by the time we make it back to Australia.

I feel like, for the first time in years, I'm truly living.

When we light the third and final round of sparklers, Jalen insists that I get one as well this time, and takes the phone off me so I can be in some photos, too. We take selfies together, the three of us squishing in with our sparklers until the lights die out.

But then no one lets go. I lower my phone and put it safely in my pocket before collecting the spent sticks and dropping them in the mug of water that's thankfully nearby. My boys lay their heads against my chest and neck, and I do the same, holding them tight.

I'm not sure what's happening, but I don't want the spell to break.

Eventually, it's Colby who speaks first.

"All I want for Christmas is you."

He says it so gently that I almost miss it over the wind. But the words cut through the noise and go straight to my heart, hope exploding like flower petals unfurling in a time lapse video. I move my head to look at him as I rub his back.

"Yeah?"

He blinks as Jalen also leans back. We're still hugging, so our faces are pretty close together, our warm breaths coming out in clouds of smoke. Colby bites his lip and looks between us. "Uh, yeah," he says like he's punch drunk. "I don't remember ever being this happy. And it's because of you guys. So thank you, I guess. I...I love you."

Now, I know that word can mean different things. There are all kinds of love. So I hold my breath and give my sweet boy time to think about what he's said.

Jalen isn't so patient.

"You know I love you too, right? Like *love* love you."

"Yeah, of course, but—" Colby says bashfully, and I can already tell he *doesn't* know.

Luckily, Jalen has been given an opening, and my little firecracker is nothing if not opportunistic.

"No, no 'buts.' I really *love* you, Colby Wilson. I moved to Australia for you."

I watch Colby with bated breath as Jalen's words sink in. "You...really...?"

Jalen glances at me. I nod, so happy for him I think I might burst. He looks back at his best friend. "Colby?" he says.

"Jalen?" Colby utters at the same time.

The matter is cleared up once and for all as Jalen's mouth crashes into Colby's.

CHAPTER 16

Jalen

*B**EY ON A BATTLESHIP!** I'M DOING IT. IT'S HAPPENING. I'M kissing my best friend!*

More importantly, he's kissing me back.

I've got one hand cupped against his face as I frantically claim his sweet, delicious mouth. The other is interlinked with Andreas's, our gloved fingers squeezing together like an anchor in a storm. That's what eventually pulls me back, gasping, and I stare at Colby in disbelief for a second.

"Did that really just happen?" I croak.

Colby swallows, already looking worried. "Is it okay?" he whispers.

I can't help the laugh that bubbles out of me, startling him. "Honey boo, I've only been dreaming about that for approximately one HUNDRED years!"

The way his pretty pink lips pop into an 'O' shape makes my heart melt. He really had no idea how crazy I've been for him all this time.

But then he gasps and looks guiltily at Andreas. "I...uh..."

Nope. Time to clear that up right away. Onto my next conquest.

"Daddy?" I say to Andreas, immediately getting both their attention. Colby is still slightly shocked, but Andreas's eyebrows shoot up, and he gives me the cutest, hopeful smile.

I think we both move at the same time, kissing eagerly. He's more confident than Colby but just as sweet from the hot chocolate. My heart flutters, and there's one heck of a party happening in my pants.

The only reason the embrace is so short is because I hear Colby gasp and can feel his anxiety coming off him in waves. So I break away from Andreas to give my bestie a big, reassuring smile.

"All *I* want for Christmas is *both* of you," I declare not only to them but all of Brighton Beach. I don't think there's anyone else around to hear me, but the beach itself knows now.

Colby looks like he can't believe what he's hearing before he turns to Andreas. "Is that what you want, sweet boy?" Andreas asks. He cups the side of Colby's face and caresses his cheek with his thumb. It's such a beautiful, tender moment it snatches my breath away.

Yes, yes, *yes*. This is exactly what I want! My Daddy and my baby boy all at the same time. *Lizzo on a life raft,* they look sooooooo good together like that.

"I…I want…" Colby squeaks, looking so afraid it breaks my heart. I lean in and nuzzle my nose against his other cold cheek.

"I think Daddy would also love a kiss from you, baby boy," I purr, my heart racing. He turns his big, blue eyes on me, and I nod in encouragement. "If that's what you want." I could be wrong, so it's important he has the opportunity to say no.

But he looks back at Andreas. They hold each other's gaze for a second. Then Colby launches forward like a rocket, kissing the crap out of Andreas right in front of me.

It's. So. HOT.

Before we lived together, I knew that Colby wasn't an overtly sexual person. I even wondered if he was ace, which I would have been okay with. I love him no matter what. But seeing the ravenous way his tongue and lips mesh with Andreas's is such a turn-on, girl, I *can't even.* My little cutie is a *sexy* baby.

He suddenly pulls away from Andreas, and before I know it, he's latched on to me again. This time he absolutely devours me, making me both moan and giggle into his mouth.

Then he pulls free once more, panting smoky breaths into the cold night air. The wind howls, and the waves crash. Mother Nature knows that this moment right here is dramatic as all hell.

"Is this real?" my boo asks so adorably.

I laugh and press our foreheads together. "If you mean that we all have mad crushes on one another and have finally stepped our pussies up to do something about it—then yes— yes, that's real." I hear Andreas laugh as he hugs us both tightly.

"My boys," he murmurs.

Look, I know I'm one for theatrics, but your girl doesn't usually lose her cool. Right there in that moment, though, I feel my eyes sting and a lump rise in my throat.

I turn my head so my and Colby's temples are still resting against each other but we're looking at Andreas. "Can we really be your boys, Daddy?"

It's my turn for him to cup the side of my face, and I melt into his touch, his gloved hand warm against my skin. "You already are, little firecracker," he says.

The new nickname makes me feel even more emotional. I sniff and try and cover it with a laugh.

"So you're...Daddy?" Colby says uncertainly.

Andreas looks uncharacteristically nervous. "Um, yeah. But only if you feel comfortable with that."

I roll my eyes. "Oh, please, Daddy-O. You've been Daddying the crap out of us ever since you met us."

He gives me a firm look, which—no, I won't lie—goes straight to my balls in a really yummy way. "That's up to Colby."

"I've been telling him he needs a Daddy for years," I say gleefully. "I always dreamed that if we got *really* lucky, we'd find Daddies who were best friends. Never in a million, billion years did I think we'd be able to *share* a dream Daddy."

Colby is shivering, and I don't think it's from the wind, because between our many layers and the Hug That's Never Going To End, it's pretty toasty in our little penguin huddle. But I can see he's struggling to believe that he deserves to be loved by not just one but two men.

"It's okay," I whisper into his ear, feeling him tremble even harder. "It's okay, I promise. You can have this. You can want this. We want you. Let us take care of you, baby boy."

"Colby," Andreas says in his delicious Daddy Dom voice, making him look up. "I treasure you. So much. I'll do whatever you want me to. If this is too much, we can slow down. But Jalen is right. It's okay for you to want this. You're a very special boy who deserves to be loved unconditionally."

That's what pushes my boo over the edge. I watch his face crumple as a sob racks his chest. He howls as he throws himself against Andreas. I wrap my body around his. I would shield him from literal ARROWS if I had to. He's my everything, and I never thought I'd get the opportunity to love him like this.

But thanks to Andreas, I might just get the chance now.

"Daddy?" he whimpers. I didn't think my heart could take much more, but that one word threatens to shatter it for all the best reasons.

"I'm here, baby boy," Andreas assures him. "Are you all right?"

He doesn't answer for a while. But his sobs settle down. Then he wipes his face with his woolen glove and takes a deep breath. "I think I'm amazing," he says with a nervous laugh.

I squeal and kiss his cheek, impossible happiness rippling through me. "Damn straight, you are."

"So…we can call you Daddy?" he asks Andreas. "Is that okay? Jalen talked to me about the sugar Daddy stuff, and I get that. He said that looking after us and paying for things makes you feel really good."

Andreas's smile is full of such adoration as he brushes the backs of his fingers against Colby's jaw. "I love it, sweetheart," he says.

"Told you," I say gently, nudging my shoulder against Colby's. He gives me a bashful look, but I do understand that he wants to get confirmation from Andreas himself. I think he's always going to need that kind of reassurance.

It's okay. I have a feeling that both I and our Daddy will be very eager to do that for him whenever he needs it.

"But is it also, um…" Colby looks mortified. So I hug him tightly to my side to give him courage. "Is it also a, um, *sexy* thing?"

He screws his eyes shut before burying his face against my neck. Oh, my sweet summer child.

Andreas laughs gently, rubbing Colby's back. "It's an everything thing to me," he explains, looking my way with a gorgeous smile. "This little troublemaker here has used it on me a few times, and I can't describe how perfect it makes me feel."

"Daddy, Daddy, Daddy," I sing happily, making Colby giggle. He lifts his head slowly, taking a breath and nibbling on his lip.

"So, we're your boys?" he asks.

My heart thunders in my chest.

"I would love that," Andreas says.

"Both of us?" Colby says. Of course he wants to double-check that. He's never felt good enough in his whole life. I'm sure he's had sex, but he's never had a boyfriend. No one's ever stood up and declared that they're picking him above anyone else.

Well, I have, but he thought I just meant as a friend. I'm going to have to work hard to change that, I'm sure.

"You're an inseparable pair," Andreas tells Colby sincerely. "It never occurred to me to pick one over the other. You're a package deal, and I couldn't have imagined a more perfect duo. You're my double trouble."

Colby whimpers, and a couple more tears spring free as he closes his eyes and rests his head on Andreas's chest. I mirror him, pressing my forehead against his again, and for a while, we all just breathe.

"Let us take care of you, little baby Coco," I murmur. I'm not even sure where the words come from, but they feel right as soon as I say them.

He blinks his eyes open to regard me with a sort of wonder. For the first time since we started hugging, he doesn't look panicked or scared by a new idea, and my heart soars.

"Little baby…?"

"Coco," I say with a nod. "Like how Andreas is Daddy, you can have a special name as well. Or something else if you don't like Coco. But you can be little with us, like a kid. We'll take care of you, okay?"

His brow furrows as he ponders my words. "I like Coco," he says, and I can't help but puff up my chest a bit with pride.

"When you're Coco, you don't have to do any adult stuff like make decisions," I tell him, warming more to the idea.

I've called him my baby boy for so long, but it wasn't until there was an actual Daddy in the picture did I understand how much age play might help him. I'm not sure if he'd want to go all in with binkies and onesies and blocks or whatever. But the whole giving up control thing? Yeah. I think that could be right up his street.

I glance at Andreas, who nods at me. I have a feeling he's been researching Daddy things online, and I'm pleased he doesn't appear put out by my suggestion. In fact, he looks like he's beaming at both of us.

"Daddy will take care of you," I continue. "And I'll help."

He licks his lips and tilts his head as he looks at me. "But what about you?"

"What about me?"

He pokes my chest. "Don't you want to be Daddied as well?"

I look between him and Andreas, who raises his eyes expectantly at me. "Oh, um, yeah. Daddying is great. But I don't think age play's really for me. I'm already a brat twenty-four seven, darling." I bat my eyelids at him. "That's my thing."

Colby huffs in an adorable little pout and pats at my chest. "But don't you want a special name, too? We're all equal in this throuple-thingy, right?"

I grin, loving how he's already calling us a throuple. "We're equal in different ways, yeah, I guess."

"Then you need a name," he says stubbornly, and my heart swells yet again.

"I love you so much," I say, shaking my head and hugging him closer to me.

Suddenly, he pulls back. "Jay Jay!" he cries triumphantly. "I can be Coco and you can be Jay Jay." He looks at Andreas. "What do you think?"

He beams at both of us. "It's up to him. How does Jay Jay sound, firecracker?"

"I love it," I say, feeling a little shy. It's a highly unusual sensation that I intend to overcome as soon as possible. "I like *both* those names very much. I like every single thing about everything that's happening right now!"

I'm yelling by the time I finish, and both of them laugh at me. My Daddy and my baby boy. My partners. My boyfriends.

"*Britney on a bike*, is this an official thing now?" I say, hamming up my shock. "Can I update my LinkedIn?"

Andreas snorts at my corny joke. "Only if I can update my Myspace," he teases right back.

"What's a Myspace?" Colby asks and I don't think he's joking.

"Oh, baby boy." I sigh happily, kissing the tip of his cold nose. "Sweet baby Coco. Please never change."

"Right," Andreas says in a booming voice. "If I'm officially Daddy now, then I'm going to take charge and insist we go back inside so I can warm you boys up."

Heat pools in my stomach, and my cock throbs in my underwear. Now I'm the one who's trembling. I'm not sure exactly what he means by that, but I have a feeling it's going to be at least a little NSFW.

"Okay, Daddy," I say.

"Yes, Daddy," Colby adds.

This feels like some kind of impossible dream. A month ago, I never would have dared imagine such a perfect scenario. But as Andreas collects up our mugs and the used sparklers, he takes Colby's hand with his free one, and I link fingers on Colby's other side.

Our improbable yet incredible trio makes our way from the beach and up the garden path to our cozy little home, ready to start the next part of our adventure.

CHAPTER 17

Colby

MY HEAD IS SPINNING. I'M EXCITED AND TERRIFIED AND IN complete disbelief that this could possibly be happening right now.

But it is.

As we spill back into the living room and shut the French doors behind us, I can't help but giggle. It's harder to deny what just happened in the light. I can see the faces of the two men I just kissed, and they're looking back at me with hunger, chests rising and falling as we gravitate toward each other again in the warmth.

Not that I'd want to deny what we did on the beach. It just seems totally unbelievable. Things like that don't happen to me.

Just like how I don't meet amazingly generous sugar Daddies who whisk me off to the other side of the world.

All these facts are very hard to refute as Andreas claims my mouth again as we stand in our holiday rental just off Brighton Beach, my skin still stinging from the cold wind. As his lips meet mine, he pulls Jalen against us, and suddenly, we're in an incredible three-way kiss. It's messy and chaotic, and I love it.

But I'm also still quite scared.

"Um," I say as I lean back and look into their dark, sparkling eyes. "How does this, uh, work? With three people?"

Andreas shrugs and grins at me. "No idea, baby boy. I've never done anything like this before."

Jalen blows a raspberry and waves his hand dismissively. "Oh, it's easy. Everyone has the parts that feel good when they're touched. You just make good use of your mouths and hands, and in the end, everyone has a good time."

My breath hitches. "You've had a threesome before?" I don't know why, but when he mentioned stuff at the club before, I always thought it was him with one other person. I suppose that's quite naïve in retrospect.

Jalen hums and plucks my bobble hat off, playing with my hair. He's been casually affectionate since he moved in with me. But now it feels completely different.

Like it's a prelude to something so much more.

"I've done lots of things before, little Coco," he purrs. God, he's so sexy. I can't believe I'm allowed to think that now!

"Oh," I say, trying not to feel intimidated. "I haven't. Done things, I mean. Uh…"

Suddenly, intimidated doesn't even cover it. I've only had sex a few times, and it was all pretty disappointing. I wasn't even sure if I enjoyed it all that much. If I couldn't please one man, how the hell am I going to satisfy *two?*

"Hey," Andreas says, rubbing my back in that perfect way he does. "Sweetheart, we don't have to do anything at all tonight. I don't want you worrying. This is supposed to be fun. I know it's all brand new and we've moved pretty fast with everything."

I take a couple of breaths and see the kindness in both his and Jalen's eyes. It helps me relax and recall Jalen's words. "Jay Jay?" I say.

He nods. "I'm right here."

"I'm…little baby Coco, yeah?"

He nods again. "If you want to be, of course."

I inhale a few more breaths. "Daddy and Jay Jay take care of baby Coco?" I utter. I feel like I'm almost dizzy. Like I'm sort of slipping away. I can hear my heartbeat so loudly in my ears and I'm hyperaware of the way both my partners are touching me. It's not bad…not at all. It's just different.

"We'll take care of everything, sweet one," Andreas assures me. "How about we get these coats off and then go to Daddy's bed for a snuggle? We can see how we feel then, okay?"

I feel myself relax, a smile slipping onto my face. "That sounds nice, Daddy," I murmur.

He kisses my forehead. "Good boy."

Jalen is grinning like an excitable kid as he pulls my gloves off and unzips my coat. Andreas pushes it off my shoulders, then kneels down and starts undoing my shoelaces.

"Oh," I say as something hits me in my chest that I wasn't expecting. Why does that feel more intimate than any sex I've ever had?

I look at Jalen and realize he's pulling off his own gloves. I scowl. That won't do. We have to take care of each other. He loves me, and I love him. So I reach out and tug the zipper on his coat.

"Coco do it," I say stubbornly.

Jalen laughs and sneaks a little peck on my lips. "Thank you, Coco," he says warmly.

Andreas helps him with his shoes as well, but he gets his own coat off before we can do anything to assist. I slip my hand against his, and so does Jalen. He looks at us like he's won the lottery.

"Hey, boys," he says softly.

"Hey, Daddy," we say in a little chorus of two. It's beautiful music to my ears.

We tug on his hands and start leading him upstairs to his bedroom. It's a little awkward on the steps, but we manage it. When we enter, the bedroom is dark, but Andreas switches on a bedside lamp so we're softly illuminated. The shadows make me feel safer. Braver.

It might be warmer inside, but despite the layers we had on, we're still chilled to the bone from standing on the beach for so long. Andreas yanks back the duvet and we all slip under the covers, still fully dressed, with him in the middle. His body feels *amazing* as he pulls us tightly to crowd either side of him. He's so big and strong, and he smells like salt air and spices.

He takes turns kissing us while Jalen and I hold hands across his stomach. We're heating up nicely under the covers, and my heartbeat is racing. This is already *so* much better than the sex I had before with those random guys. I think the big difference is that I didn't know them. Whereas Jalen is my best friend in the whole wide world, and no one has even taken care of me the way Andreas has these past few weeks. Maybe to me someone can't just look sexy for me to be attractive. I need to know their souls as well.

Jalen and Andreas have heavenly souls, I decide. Like angels.

I wriggle, and Andreas laughs at me. "What is it, little one?"

"I, um, feel, um…"

Jalen laughs too and kisses me right in front of Andreas's face. "Are you feeling sexy, little baby? Do you want us to touch you?"

I might have realized something about what turns me on, but that doesn't make me any less experienced in this moment. I feel my cheeks flame, and I hide my face against Andreas's neck with a whimper. Both my partners hug me and murmur nice words.

"It's okay to want that, sweetheart," Andreas says, his voice like syrup. "I want that too."

"For us to touch you?" I say, lifting my head.

For some reason, that doesn't seem quite as scary, even though I was always terrified of doing anything with the guys I slept with in the past. But I didn't know them. I was afraid they'd tell me off for doing it wrong. Andreas would never, *ever* do that. More than that, I suddenly really want to make him feel good. I want to show him how much I like him and how much he means to me.

"I meant that I want to touch you, baby boy," Andreas says with a crooked eyebrow. "But, uh, I guess you've got a different idea?"

He laughs as I grope him clumsily through his jeans. Jalen gasps and lifts the covers to see what's happening. "You're having a party without me!" he shrieks.

But we're both laughing as he attacks Andreas's fly, and he's got no hesitations as he fishes his hand inside Andreas's underwear. In a flash, the mood changes from giggly to sensual, and I love it.

I kiss Andreas's neck as my best friend and I push down his clothes to completely free his cock. He moans as we stroke it. It's so big in my hand. Jalen moves down to fondle his balls as well, and Andreas makes such filthy sounds I feel dizzy.

"Good boys," he murmurs, his eyelids heavy as he switches between kissing both of our mouths. "You're so gorgeous. My good boys."

With a devilish look in his eyes, Jalen disappears under

the covers. I feel rather than see his lips wrapping around Andreas's shaft, his hand linking with mine as we hold the base. Andreas arches his back and hisses in pleasure, gritting his teeth.

"Fuck!"

I hug him tighter, kissing along his jawline. "It's okay, Daddy," I say, feeling more confident in bed than I ever have in my life. "We're here. We're taking care of you now."

He thrusts his fingers through the hair on the back of my head and crushes his mouth against mine in the filthiest kiss I've ever experienced. It's raw and aggressive as our teeth clash. My lips throb as much as my dick, and I'm very quickly gasping for breath between assaults.

"Jay Jay!" he grunts in a warning, but my bestie doesn't let up. I can't believe after being friends with him for years and years, I'm in a bed with him, pleasuring another man together. It's the hottest, most awesome feeling ever.

God, I wonder if he'll blow *me*. Maybe not tonight, but it seems entirely likely that it's something he might want to do in the near future.

I almost come in my pants just thinking about it.

I'm pulled from my thoughts as Andreas gashes his teeth and convulses, his orgasm slamming into him. He looks so gorgeous I can't really believe it. I feel so privileged that I get to see him like that.

After several seconds, he gasps, taking in deep breaths. Jalen reappears, his hair completely askew and his lips swollen and red as he grins like he just won first prize in the blow job Olympics.

"Did you like that, Daddy?" he asks saucily.

Andreas grabs the back of his neck and gives him the same sort of obscene kiss he gave me. It's super hot, and I'm reminded that I've still got my own not-so-little problem in my underwear.

Andreas hasn't forgotten, though, because he's an amazing Daddy who takes care of his boys.

Once he's got his breath back, he hugs us to his chest for a few moments. I'm so warm now in all my clothes, but I kind of like being a bit overheated after freezing on the beach. The sweat makes the air taste and smell so good. I feel almost feral, like an animal.

"Kiss for me," Andreas says hoarsely. His pupils are blown, and he looks wild. A shiver runs over my body as I look at Jalen and realize that our Daddy wants us to kiss for him. He wants to *watch* us.

No one's ever looked at me the way Andreas is looking at me right now.

I lick my lips and lean in, not nervous, just excited that I get to kiss my best friend again. I still can't quite believe that he feels the same way about me. All these years, I was suffering alone with no idea that he was in the same boat.

I'm so glad we met Andreas and he gave us the push we needed to finally admit how we feel. I'm glad we met Andreas for so many reasons. He's amazing all by himself.

All of a sudden, I jerk in surprise. So does Jalen, and we laugh at each other before looking at Andreas, who has obviously put his hands on both our crotches. He arches an eyebrow, looking stern. I don't know why that's hot, but it really, *really* is.

"Did I tell you to stop kissing?" he growls.

My stomach flips, and my cock jumps in my jeans against his palm. "S-sorry, Daddy," I whisper.

Jalen laughs, then moans wantonly. "Sorry, Daddy," he says, not sounding sorry at all.

But he does start kissing me again with even more heat. It's slow and possessive, making my heart race and my arms tremble where they're holding me up over Andreas's chest.

It's clumsy, but it doesn't matter. All I care about is that

Andreas's fingers somehow manage to undo my jeans and shove them down along with my underwear. He gets his palm wrapped around my shaft, and I guess he does the same to Jalen as we're soon moaning into each other's mouths. I'm so sensitive from not having sex in ages and being crazily turned on. I'm leaking heaps of precum, which just helps his hand glide even better along my slick shaft.

I'm making a high-pitched squealing noise as Jalen mashes his mouth against mine like he's trying to eat me whole. "Good boys," Andreas rasps, sounding totally wrecked. "So perfect. Come for Daddy."

Those words send me hurtling over the edge. This is the most outrageous, sexiest, filthiest, hottest thing I've done by a million miles, and I come harder than I ever have in my entire life.

Jalen reaches out and grabs the back of my neck, pressing our foreheads together as he starts to come as well. I've never felt closer to him. But I realize to my horror that I'm crying before I've even finished spilling my load. My head is spinning, and I'm struggling for air.

"It's okay, little baby," Jalen gasps, hugging me to him. Then Andreas's strong arms envelop us as he drags us down to his chest. Our clothes and the sheets are a mess, but none of that matters as his voice rumbles through my body.

"I've got you, little one. Oh, my good, perfect, beautiful boys. Daddy's here. It's okay."

I'm still shaking and hiccuping, but his words cut through all my emotions, and I believe him.

It's okay.

For the first time in probably my entire life, I know with my whole heart that things really are okay because I have my Daddy and my Jay Jay wrapped tightly in my arms.

I never want to let them go.

CHAPTER 18

Andreas

WHEN I WAKE THE NEXT MORNING, IT TAKES ME SEVERAL seconds to orient myself. Like the day before, I struggle to recognize that I'm not in my own bedroom for a moment. But then everything else comes crashing down like the waves on Brighton Beach.

My boys.

Why aren't they here?

I blink, suddenly very aware as both my hands reach out under the covers and find no one with me. My heart rate picks up. I know we all fell asleep together. I was a mean Daddy and made my boys go back to their room to change into their pajamas while I quickly swapped the bottom sheet over with a fresh one I'd found in a cupboard. I've even made them brush their teeth. The upside of them dragging their feet about it was that I had time to put both the sheet and our messy clothes in the washing machine. But then we'd all snuggled together, falling into a deep sleep.

So deep I didn't feel them leave.

I glance at the clock. It's half past seven, and from what I can see beyond the curtains, the sun is just starting to peek over the horizon, making the sky pretty colors.

It's also Christmas Day.

It's a long time since I felt any kind of excitement to wake up on December twenty-fifth. But despite my concerns, I do feel some fluttering in my belly. I might not know exactly what's going on right this second, but I know without a doubt that last night was one of the best of my entire life. There's no reason why today shouldn't be incredible as well.

I take a breath and reason that everything is probably fine. So I throw on some jogging bottoms and a T-shirt before brushing my teeth. The heating is on, but I still find some socks and a hoodie as well, wanting to feel cozy. Finally, I exit the bedroom, on the hunt for my boys.

I hear the giggling from downstairs almost right away, and my heart soars. See, everything *is* fine. They're just up to trouble, and that's a-okay by me. I grin as I jog downward, not sure what to expect.

The sight that greets me makes me stop a few steps from the bottom, where I can see over the banister into the living room. I gasp and touch my hand to my chest as a lump rises in my throat, and my eyes prickle with tears.

Those boys.

"Merry Christmas!" they yell when they see me, throwing their arms in the air. They've got their ugly Christmas jumpers over their PJs, but that's not what startled me. Of course I'm always more than happy to see them. But it's what they've done for me that's so incredibly touching.

There's tinsel draped everywhere. On the artwork hanging from the walls, on the TV, even in a circle around the coffee table. One of those banners made from individual letters strung together is also on the wall, tied between two light fittings, spelling 'HAPPY HOLIDAYS!' I didn't know Christmas balloons were a thing, but there are a couple dozen bouncing around the house filled with sparkles that read 'Ho ho ho!' Confetti shaped like snowflakes has been strewn over every surface. I'm sure that's going to be fun to clean up at some point, but right now, I couldn't give a toss.

I don't think anyone has ever done anything so sweet for me in my adult life. I'm reminded of how my mum would always try and surprise me on my birthday growing up. Even if it was just a cake from Tesco, she always wanted me to know it was my special day.

That's exactly how I feel right now.

Special.

"What's all this?" I say thickly with a laugh as I make it down the last few steps.

They both rush over to me and throw their arms around me. "We smuggled it all from back home!" Jalen says gleefully.

"Do you like it?" Colby asks, his voice tinged with anxiety. I understand that he's probably always going to be a little worried about doing anything for anyone, having had his spirit crushed all his life. But how he could think this is anything other than incredible is still a bit heartbreaking.

"Like it?" I cry incredulously. "I *love* it! This is the best Christmas *ever.*"

Jalen tuts and rolls his eyes. "We haven't even given you your presents yet, Daddy," he says with a mischievous air.

I crease my brow at him. "Presents? You already did all this. You didn't need to get me presents as well."

"They're not much," Colby says quickly. "Just silly things."

"Silly but fabulous!" Jalen declares as he tugs on my hand. "Come on, come on!"

I laugh and shake my head, feeling less guilty about my own little surprise now. "Hang on a second. I need to go get something from my suitcase. Why don't you put the kettle on and maybe some Christmas music?"

Jalen twirls on the spot as Colby heads into the kitchen. "Yessss!" says Jalen. "I made my own playlist with Mariah and Kelly and Ariana and Christina!"

I tilt my head at him. "No Dean Martin?"

He scrunches his nose at me. "Was he in Take That?"

I drop my head back and laugh as I pull him in for a cuddle and kiss the top of his head. "I'll settle for some Wham! instead, okay?"

"Okay, Daddy," he says sweetly. "I can add some George Michael, just for you."

Not wanting to miss a moment with my beautiful boys, I rush upstairs and find what I'm looking for, hidden away in my suitcase where the boys wouldn't accidentally see. I also fetch a couple of things from my backpack that I took with us to the pier yesterday.

The stockings were already reasonably full, but I add the stuffed animals to the top of each of them, then squeeze in a stick of classic Brighton rock down the sides. That's basically just rainbow-colored sugar, but it's the holidays, and my boys deserve all the treats.

"Merry Christmas!" I cry, holding them up as I re-emerge down the stairs. My boys are waiting patiently on the sofa, and my heart leaps as their faces light up at their presents.

"You made us stockings?" Jalen squeals. Colby doesn't speak, but his eyes shimmer with tears. I wonder if he'll ever move past feeling he's not worthy of being spoiled.

I know I'm not going to get tired of spoiling him anytime soon, that's for sure.

"Those are the teddies you won at the pier yesterday, I know," I explain sheepishly. "But they looked so cute poking their heads out of the top like that, I wanted to gift them to you again."

I lay each stocking over the correct boy's lap, kissing them gently on the head as I do. I went to a special place in

Sydney and paid a slightly ridiculous amount of money to get their names printed on them, along with a pattern of snowflakes, candy canes, and reindeer. At the time I wondered if it was too much.

Now, it doesn't feel like enough.

"Thank you, Daddy," Colby manages to whisper. Jalen is already pulling things out of his, but I stop him.

"Ah! Wait a second, firecracker. Let Daddy get a cup of tea and the mince pies. Then we can all open them together."

Jalen pouts, but he also stops what he's doing. "Fine. Does that mean you also have a stocking?"

I shake my head. "No, but I want to watch you guys."

"You should have one as well, Daddy," Colby protests.

He's so adorable. I kiss the top of his head again as I stand, going to the kitchen. "It's okay, sweetheart. Maybe next year."

I realize what I've said and pause for just a fraction before continuing to walk into the other room. That's a long way off, and who knows where we'll be in a year's time.

On the other hand, I feel perfectly confident that this is just the beginning of our really beautiful relationship, so why not daydream about next Christmas?

Not that I want to wish away *this* Christmas. It's only just getting started, after all.

Thanks to Colby the kettle is already boiled, so I make myself tea and the boys another hot chocolate and marshmallow special. There's a tray by the microwave, so I grab that to place the mugs on along with the pack of six mince pies that I've been saving. Cake still isn't an ideal breakfast, but it's slightly better than seaside rock.

My heart melts when I turn around back into the living room. Jalen has his arms around Colby's back in a possessive manner while Colby hugs around Jalen's waist. They're kissing sweetly until they sense my presence.

"Oops," Jalen says with a giggle. "Sorry, Daddy."

"You never, *ever*, have to apologize for that," I say with a light-hearted scoff as I place the tray down amid the confetti and tinsel.

"Why did you never say anything?" Colby blurts out, looking at Jalen with wide eyes.

Jalen looks confused as he brushes back a blond lock of Colby's hair. "Because you need a Daddy, silly. I've told you that all along. I'm not a Daddy. But I'm a pretty great Daddy's assistant." He flashes a grin, but then he frowns at Colby. "Besides, you never said a thing, either."

Colby blushes and tries to make himself smaller. "Because you're far too fabulous for me," he mumbles, and my heart breaks. I wondered if it was something like that.

Jalen's jaw drops. "What?" he shrieks. "Are you insane? You are the most perfect little boo-boo boyfriend anyone could ever wish for!"

Colby's shaking his head, so I reach over and squeeze his knee, snapping him out of it. "Little one," I say softly. "Jalen doesn't need another Jalen. Do you think the world could cope with that?"

That startles a laugh out of him, which was my intention. But I'm also correct. Even Jalen knows it. "This is it, right here," he says, waving his hands at me. "Daddy-O has all the facts."

"You know they say opposites attract for a reason," I continue kindly. "The only thing getting in your way was you guys."

But Colby frowns and shakes his head as he grabs my hand. "No, Daddy. We needed you to bring us together. That's how this works the best. All three of us are just as important as each other."

I sigh happily as I look at him and then Jalen, who has his hands on his chest and gives me a dramatic little nod. "These are also facts," he says sweetly. "We needed a Daddy. I thought that meant a Daddy each, but sharing is a million, billion times better."

I couldn't agree more.

"There we go," I say, closing the matter. "No more worrying about that. We're all in this together. Equal partners, boyfriends, a family, however you want to call it."

"Those all sound good, Daddy," Colby says shyly.

I grin, then place a mug of hot chocolate on the table in front of each boy and open up the mince pies. "Come on, then. These are for you, and I think it's past stocking time."

Jalen squeals and attacks his one, having already pulled out his shark from yesterday. Along with the hard rock candy are the things I sourced back in Sydney. Mostly they're silly things like mini notepads with sparkly rainbows on the cover and cat-themed socks. I also got them each a pack of cheap plastic dinosaurs that obviously aren't from Jurassic Galaxy, but these ones all have Santa hats on.

That makes them howl with laughter, and Jalen immediately jumps up to start placing them all over the living room among their other decorations. Colby, though, comes over to me. I think he intended to perch on the arm of the squishy chair I'm sitting on, but I pull him into my lap. He giggles, then immediately tucks against me, his small, soft body feeling so good against mine.

"It's time for your presents now, Daddy," he says.

"Yes!" Jalen cries, spinning and jumping like he's a ballerina. "I'll go get them! You two stay there."

That's fine by me.

"I need my laptop!" Colby calls out after him.

"Will do," Jalen yells back, already on his way.

As he charges up the stairs, I nuzzle my nose against Colby's cheek before capturing his mouth in a sweet little kiss.

"Is that all right?" he whispers, looking up at me with wide eyes. "Without Jalen."

I rub his side soothingly. "I think we should all feel free to touch each other whenever we want. We're all equal, remember?"

He bites his lip, but he's smiling. "Okay, Daddy."

A wolf whistle makes us look up and laugh. Jalen is jogging back down the stairs with Colby's old laptop as well as a very messily wrapped present. It's basically a lump of screwed-up Christmas paper with about twenty bows stuck onto it.

"I tried," Jalen says with a wince as he hands it to me. Colby shifts so he's sitting more upright and takes his laptop from Jalen, who perches next to me on the arm of the chair.

"Baby, it's the thought that counts," I tell Jalen earnestly.

He snorts. "So you agree it looks like a car crash."

I hum. "No comment," I say with a wink.

He huffs and crosses his arms dramatically. "Just open it already, Mean Daddy!"

Of course I'm only teasing, so I lean up, seeking a kiss, which he gives me. Bloody hell. What a difference a day makes. I can't believe I can just kiss these gorgeous boys now whenever we want.

The sticky tape is wound around several times, so in the end, I give up and use my teeth to rip it. Colby is giggling like mad, and Jalen is still acting like he's sulking, but I can see his lips twitching in a smile as well.

Once I free the gift, though, my jaw drops as I realize what he's done.

It's a photo multi-frame, but he's hand-decorated it with glitter and seashells. "I got them from our mini Christmas Day on Manly Beach," he says excitedly as he points at the different shells. "I wanted you to have something personal to put up in your apartment. I wasn't sure what photos you might want to use, but now I was thinking maybe ones from this trip?"

I swallow the lump in my throat and hug him to me. "That's so incredibly thoughtful, little firecracker," I say, thinking of the log flume picture and all the selfies from the pier and the beach. We'll need to take more today in our Christmas jumpers, perhaps wearing paper hats from our crackers. I never want to forget our first day together in an official relationship.

"Okay, Coco's turn!" Jalen says gleefully. "Why did you need your laptop?"

Colby looks scared again, his brow furrowed as he bites his lip, his gaze skittering between the two of us. "It's okay if you don't like it," he says quietly. "It's silly."

"Baby boy," I admonish. "If it's from you, I already know I'll love it."

He takes a deep breath before cracking open his laptop. His finger whizzes over the mouse pad as he brings something up, then holds out the computer for us to see.

It's a lot of writing. At the top is a title: 'Merry Spacemas.' I glance down and start reading the bulk of the text.

My jaw drops as Jalen shrieks.

"Is this...?" I utter.

"Have you written us a self-insert Jurassic Galaxy fanfiction?" Jalen asks at a pitch I'm sure only dogs can normally hear.

Colby nods, still looking anxious.

I've never read fanfiction before, so I'm a bit slow on the uptake. But I think I understand. "You've written a story featuring us three with the characters of the TV show?"

"Um, yes," Colby says. "It's just a bit of fluff, so there's not much plot. I made us friends of the gang, and we're visiting for Christmas."

For a second, I'm not sure what to say. "This is incredibly thoughtful and creative, baby boy."

"My boo-boo is a genius," Jalen says smugly. "I can't wait to read it. Ooh! Is it a *naughty* fic?"

Colby's face goes Father Christmas red. "No!" he squeaks.

Jalen arches an eyebrow. "Okay, but could you add a chapter two that *is?*"

I bellow out a laugh. "You boys," I say, leaning over to kiss Colby sensually on the lips. "I love it so much, little one."

"You haven't even read it yet," he mumbles shyly, but he's finally smiling.

"I don't need to, although I'm looking forward to it. Just the idea is the sweetest thing ever." I turn to Jalen. "Both your gifts are incredible."

Jalen shakes his head and laughs. "Colby's is *way* better, but that's okay."

I grab his jumper and drag him down so I can kiss him hard. When I release him, he's panting, and his eyes are glassy. "I love them *both,*" I say firmly.

"Uh-huh," Jalen says, sounding woozy. Then he gives me a wicked grin before flicking his eyebrows at Colby. "We don't have to leave for a while, right? How about we go upstairs and enact chapter two ourselves?"

I bite my lip and hold both my boys tighter. "I like the sound of that *very much.*"

CHAPTER 19

Jalen

I'm like a kid at Christmas.

Oh, wait. It *is* Christmas.

Lucky me.

I grab Colby's hand and pull him off the armchair. "Catch us, Daddy!" I cry, my heart racing as the two of us run giggling across the living room and up the stairs. "Wait," I say as we reach the landing, then yank Colby into our bedroom instead of Andreas's.

"What are you doing?" Colby asks breathlessly. "Daddy already washed the bedsheet last night. It should be dry by now. We're fine to, um, make another mess in his room on the new one."

"Oh, don't you worry," I say as I dive into my case. "I just want to make even more of a mess."

With a flourish, I pull out a bottle of lubricant and a box of condoms. Colby gasps. "You *packed* those?"

I jump back up to my feet and grab his hand again. "Oh, baby. A girl can hope. And look! It paid off!"

I can hear Daddy still making his way up the stairs, so we dash into the bedroom ahead of him.

He growls like a bear, and I swear my cock almost leaps out of my pajamas all by itself.

"Have you boys been naughty or nice?" Andreas booms.

"Nice!" Colby yells back at the same time I shout, "Naughty!" I toss the supplies onto the nightstand before dragging him onto the bed with me. I notice that Andreas has laid a blanket over the duvet, and I can't help but think that was on purpose to help with any clean-up later.

Colby is shaking as I cuddle him to me, both of us on our knees. I won't lie. I'm trembling in anticipation as well.

Andreas saunters into the room, oozing sexiness. He moves like a jungle cat, and I feel like we're little mice caught in his sights. The thrill is exhilarating.

I don't take my eyes off him, but I fling my hand out toward the nightstand. "I got you another present, Daddy," I say breathlessly.

He gets to the bed and walks on his knees up the mattress until he reaches us. In one smooth motion, he slips his hands under our jumpers, caressing our tummies and making us shiver. He nuzzles his head between ours, first kissing Colby's neck and then mine.

"And what did you want to do with the condoms and lube, little firecracker?" he rumbles in my ear.

"Uhh," I say, squirming against his ticklish touch. "Play with them, Daddy. Play with us." He hums, but I'm not quite sure he gets that I really, *really* need more from him this time. "Your girl here is totally versatile, in case you were wondering. She'll catch and pitch. Just thought that might help with any logistical planning going on."

Andreas laughs and nips at my earlobe. "Thank you, naughty boy. How about you, nice boy? If we take things a little further, do you have any preferences?"

"Um, yeah," Colby says. I squeeze his side, giving him support to be brave and ask for what he wants. "I just bottom, please. Thank you. Did you want to, uh, do that now?"

Andreas moves to capture his mouth. Honestly, as much as I want to be in on all the action, watching those two make out is just…*urgh!* Delicious.

"It's a rule, baby boy," Andreas says against Colby's lips, "now and forever, that you never have to do anything you're not comfortable with. That you're not excited by. You never have to justify yourself or anything. You simply say 'yes' or 'no'—understood?"

Colby sighs, looking just a little relieved. "Okay, Daddy. I understand."

"Good boy."

"So what *are* we doing?" I ask with a grin, not afraid to get a little bratty when my dick is making such an obvious tent in my jammies.

"Hmm," Andreas says, pretending to mull it over. "I reckon the next thing we should try is…getting naked. Thoughts?"

"P!nk on a pedestal, yessss," I hiss. But then I look over at Colby. "Naked?"

He gulps and takes a breath. "Yes," he agrees with conviction.

I lean over and kiss him. I could tell him how many millions of ways I've pictured him with no clothes on over the years, but that might intimidate him. I want to reassure him, not add any pressure.

"You're so beautiful," is what I say instead. "Our little baby Coco. Can Daddy and Jay Jay help? We'll take care of everything. You just relax."

"That's a good idea, firecracker," Andreas says, placing a kiss on the side of my neck. "Just relax, baby boy. We got this."

He takes his hand off my stomach and concentrates on

lifting Colby's sweater and pajama top off in one motion. Then he gently pushes him to lie down, so I flop beside him and distract him with a kiss. I realize I said that both Daddy *and* I would look after him, but so far Andreas is doing all the leg work. Well, I can be the dazzling entertainment in that case.

"I love you," I whisper between kisses, skimming my hand over his chest. "I have for so long. I can't believe I get to touch you like this. I'm so lucky."

"I'm the lucky one," he insists. He looks from me to Andreas with a gasp as Andreas lifts his hips and pulls down Colby's pajama bottoms.

Then *Rihanna on a rhino*, I can see his cock. It's so beautiful. Actually, it's bigger than I'd expected, and my mouth waters thinking about getting my hands or lips on it. The head is red and shiny with excitement. I bet it tastes delectable.

"Your turn," Andreas says, and that's all the warning I get before he pounces on me. I shriek and wriggle as he straddles my hips, first yanking off my top and sweater, then his own T-shirt. He's got a solid, hairy chest. I reach up and run my hands over his pecs with a groan.

He wastes no time in tugging down my pants, getting me all naked, too. Then he stands at the foot of the bed and shoves off his sweatpants and socks.

After that, there's nothing between the three of us except acres of glorious skin.

He crawls back over us, his hard cock swinging between us as he leans down for another messy three-way kiss. They might be a bit impractical, but they're becoming my favorite thing, like, ever, *ever*. I reach up to fondle his length that I swallowed down last night to completion. I'm happy to see it in Technicolor this morning after only really feeling it under the covers last night.

He moans, but then he's moving back down the bed, alternating between kissing each of our chests.

My breath hitches when I suspect what his destination is.

I grab Colby's hand and kiss the back of it, looking into his eyes at the moment Andreas swallows him down. Colby gasps and squeezes my hand tight. I bite my lip and grunt as Andreas slips his hand over my shaft, rubbing his thumb along the leaking slit, using the precum to lubricate as he starts stroking me.

"Oh, *wow*," I utter, not taking my eyes off my best friend's face. This is so erotic I feel like I'm going to shatter right there and then. Our hot, sugary-sweet Daddy is touching me and Colby at the same time, pleasuring us both as we gaze into each other's eyes.

It's too much. I lean forward and capture Colby's mouth for a deep kiss, our tongues tangling as Andreas undoes us.

Without warning, though, he lets me go. Before I can protest vocally, let alone look, he's wrapped his lips around my length, swallowing me all the way. I drop my head back and wail, clinging to Colby's hand. He gnashes his teeth beside me, and I can only assume Andreas is now jerking him off instead.

Whitney on a windsurfer, his mouth is so hot and wet as he sucks and swallows and drives me insane. I can feel myself start to peak, but of course that's when he pops off with an evil grin.

"*Da-dee!*" I screech in protest.

He moves up the bed to capture my mouth and run my lower lip between his teeth. "You're so gorgeous, firecracker," he says huskily. Then he leans over and gives Colby a sweeter kiss, but it's still intense. "So beautiful. My perfect pair. Daddy wants to watch you again. Shall we make a mess?"

My toes curl in pure pleasure, and my heart flutters excitedly. "Tell us what to do, Daddy," I rasp.

"Daddy wants to watch his baby boys kiss and touch and come. Help each other. Because you love each other, don't you, sweet boys?"

Colby reaches his hand out to cup my face and looks longingly into my eyes. "Yes, I love you," he affirms.

"I love you, too," I say. I don't think I'll ever get tired of being allowed to say that out loud now.

"Good boys," Andreas says, stroking his own length. "Show Daddy how much you love each other."

I shiver, overwhelmed with lust. Is he going to *come all over us?* Like an animal marking its territory? *Urgh,* I want a stamp on my forehead that says 'PROPERTY OF ANDREAS LAU' for heaven's sake. But I'll take getting sprayed with his seed for now.

Maybe I'll beg for him to give us love bites later.

Wrapping my hand around Colby's pretty cock feels like a sort of homecoming. As if his body has always belonged to me, because I know mine has always belonged to him. I might have played with a lot of people, but it's always Colby I've thought of. He has my heart, so it would make sense he'd also have my body and soul.

Equally, him touching my cock is utterly glorious. I cry out against his mouth, his breath lingering with mine. I press my free hand to his chest, feeling his heart beating against my palm.

"Coco," I utter like his name is a prayer. "Baby. Love you."

"Jay Jay," he murmurs back at me. We're looking at each other through our lashes as we chase our climaxes. I feel like I'm flying.

What makes it even more incredible as we frantically jerk each other off is hearing Andreas's grunts from where he's kneeling above us. His hand squelches over his cock, making me think that he lubed up to make it feel even more awesome. He's watching us like a dirty video on the internet and, girl, I *love* it.

We're his boys. He's claiming us like a caveman dragging us back to his lair.

"Daddy," I say. *"Coco."*

With their names on my lips, I let go. Last night was amazing, but this is even better as my orgasm rips through me, blinding me and robbing the breath from my lungs. As I scream, I feel Colby grip tightly onto my hand, hot cream spurting all over my hand.

Struggling for air, I lightly kiss my baby boy, then manage to turn my head enough to look at Andreas. He's utterly debauched as his hand flies over his swollen cock, his eyelids heavy as he continues to watch us.

I bring my sticky hand up and lick Colby's mess from my fingertips. "Come all over us, Daddy," I whisper. "We're yours."

His entire body shudders, and he drops his head back as he strokes even faster. Within seconds, he's splattering all over me and Colby, bellowing to the heavens above. Colby's eyes flutter shut as some of the seed hits his face, and in some twisted way, he's never looked more angelic to me in our lives.

There's nothing more pure or innocent than the way he's trusted the both of us to take care of him. We said we would, and we did.

When Andreas has wrung himself dry, he collapses on top of us and hugs us both like he's clinging to life through our bodies. We giggle and squeal and complain that he's heavy, but the truth is it's a sweaty, goopy, blissful mess. Like a fingerpainting that accidentally turned into a masterpiece.

I couldn't wish for a better Christmas present if I tried.

CHAPTER 20

Andreas

How is it that the hottest sex I've ever had was also the sweetest? These boys, I swear.

I was being honest the night before when I said that I wasn't sure how it worked with three people in a bed. That's not something I've ever done before or even really thought much about. But with these two in my arms, it becomes natural. I know that I just want to see them and be with them. To pleasure them and guide them.

And it doesn't hurt that Jalen has apparently had group sex more than once before. Kinky little minx.

My kinky little minx.

But seeing them both touching each other like that was both so beautiful and incredibly erotic. I'm glad we're not rushing to extremes for Colby's sake, but I'm also glad Jalen is committed to taking care of him just as much as I am. Like a sexy mentor, coaxing the very best out of Colby's gorgeous body.

I could have lain on that bed all morning, just trailing my hands over both their forms, memorizing every perfect inch of them. Alas, we have places to be. Namely, my family will be expecting us in an hour or two for Christmas brunch and present opening. So I'd better be responsible.

Sometimes it sucks to be Daddy.

I gently cajole the boys off the mattress, extremely thankful that I thought to put a blanket down before we had our fun. That can go straight into the wash, and so can we.

This time, though, we all bundle into the big bathroom together.

Jalen is still giddy as I get the shower going. He keeps kissing Colby and running his hands up and down his flanks, making our baby boy giggle. I'm grateful for this modern holiday rental, as instead of a weak stream over an old bathtub, we've got a walk-in rainfall shower that's *just* big enough for three people.

"Come on now, boys," I say as I usher them under the water.

I already checked there were some products there. They look quite extensive, so I assume that most of them are Jalen's. I usually make do with an all-in-one gel for both body and hair, but Jalen has different bottles for face, body, shampoo, and conditioner.

He grabs Colby's hand and squeezes a little face wash onto his fingers. I chuckle as my firecracker fusses over our baby boy. In the meantime, I drizzle shampoo onto both their heads, then take turns massaging the products in.

It all just feels so natural. Like everything with these two, I suppose. I've showered with boyfriends after sex before, but we generally just did our own thing or went for round two. But the boys let me wash them in such an intimate way it stirs up emotions in me in a completely different way than in the bedroom. They're really allowing me to take care of them.

Once we're all dried off, they insist on wearing their Christmas jumpers again. I think they'll probably be all right for one more day, but tomorrow I'm going to sneak them away from the boys and bung them into the wash. I'm sure we'll have dirtied more sheets by then so I can justify another round of laundry.

The thought of going again makes my cock twitch, and I smirk to myself. I might not be in my twenties anymore, but I can already tell that these boys are going to keep me on my toes as if I am.

Sometime later, we're finally out the door and in another Uber. If I thought my parents' house was chaos before, it's absolute madness when we arrive at a little after eleven o'clock. The driveway is so full of cars that our Uber has to drop us off in the street. When we ring the bell, I'm not sure if anyone even hears it.

Eventually, the door opens…and no one's there. That is until I drop my gaze to see the tiny princess standing on her tiptoes to reach the handle. She staggers away from the door and brandishes a sparkly wand with a star on the end at us, shoving a tiara and a mop of dark hair away from her face.

"Berry Mistmas!" the toddler shrieks, shaking the wand at us.

"Chloe!" a panicked voice comes from the hallway.

In a flash, my cousin, Lou, has scooped up the child into her arms, alarmedly scanning the faces before her. Obviously, she doesn't recognize Jalen or Colby, but then she clocks me and breaks into a relieved smile.

"Andy!" she cries, throwing her free arm around my neck. "Your mum said you'd surprised them. It's *so* nice to see you. How long's it been?"

I point at the mini terror on her hip who is currently bopping me on the head with her wand. "Long enough that this is our first meeting," I say jovially.

Lou sighs and steps away so I'm out of the danger zone.

"Chloe, no," she says. "That's not kind. This is Cousin Andy. We like him."

"Dee-Dee!" she yells, bouncing up and down.

"Close enough," I tell her with a wink. Then I move back and put my hands on my boys' lower backs. "These are my friends from Australia, Jalen and Colby. Guys, this is my cousin Lou and her daughter Chloe. Lou and I used to get into all kinds of trouble when we were growing up."

She gasps as she steps aside to let us in. "I was a *saint*," she says in mock outrage. "You were the bad boy."

"And don't we believe you," Jalen says with a nod before holding out a finger to Chloe. "Now this looks like a very good little princess. I love your tiara! Can I try it on?"

She frowns at Jalen for a second before yelling "NO" and smacking him on the head with her wand.

"Chloe!" Lou yelps in horror, but we're all laughing.

"They call it the terrible twos for a reason," I remind her.

Chloe has started crying, and Lou gives me a withering look. "You'll earn the right to give me parenting advice when and *only* when you become a parent yourself. Until then, zip it, mister."

She gives me a triumphant grin, then hurries off, presumably to give her daughter to an auntie so she can replace her with a glass of wine.

I glance at my boys, who are both only just containing themselves. "No," I say firmly even though I'm grinning. "She doesn't mean that kind of Daddy."

They're both still cackling as they take their shoes and coats off when Anisha comes out of the bustling kitchen and sees us. "You made it!" she cries like it's more of a surprise than when we trekked it from Australia. "Merry Christmas." She hugs and kisses all of us. "Brunch is nearly served. Dad's made a pile of eggs. There's loads of salmon and an entire tower of bagels. Help yourself to a mimosa, too."

Jalen's face lights up. "I don't mind if I do!" He grabs Colby's hand, and they both run into the thick of it.

"Oh, I should go introduce them to people, so they don't think there are strangers in the house," I fret, thinking of baby Chloe.

But Anisha places a hand on my chest to stop me, her long, sparkly Christmas nails looking a little menacing. "They can introduce themselves, baby bro," she says mischievously. "The question is, who are they going to introduce themselves *as?*"

"Jalen and Colby," I say without missing a beat.

She rolls her eyes. "Who are they *to you*, Andreas?"

I can't help but smile. I tried to change from Andy to Andreas when I left uni, but she's the only one who really listened to me. It doesn't help that it's much easier to say 'Uncle Andy' than it is 'Uncle Andreas.' However, I appreciate her making the effort.

"I…"

My sister sighs. "You said you paid for all your flights here with air miles. But you need to *go places* to get air miles, and those things expire. Bro, you're a hermit. You paid for the trip up front, didn't you? Three business class flights for you and your *just friends.*" She arches an eyebrow, calling me out on my bullshit.

I deflate. I can't lie to her, and I don't want to. "I think they're sort of everything to me," I say, throwing up my hands in defeat.

She softens and pats my chest. "Since when?"

"Since the moment I met them," I joke, even though I'm actually half-serious. "But technically…since last night."

Her jaw drops. "Are you serious? Things changed last night?"

I shake my head, still not *quite* believing it. "Everything changed, yeah. Nish, they're so wonderful."

"But?" she asks with a crooked eyebrow. Because she's my sister and of course she can sense there's a 'but' lurking just below the surface.

"But...is it weird that there are two of them? And they're younger than me?"

She scowls at me for a second before hitting my shoulder, and not lightly.

"Ow?" I say accusingly.

She just smirks. "Talk shit, get hit," she informs me like we're suddenly teenagers again and she really does know everything that I don't.

"But—"

"But nothing," she interrupts. "You're all consenting adults. You're all adorable together. And you've always loved taking care of people. Your other boyfriends never let you, though. If you ask me, even from a glance, this seems like the healthiest relationship you've ever had."

I open and close my mouth. However, I find I have nothing to argue back with.

"It's very early days," I say instead, trying to deflect some of her enthusiasm that's quite frankly a little scary. I have no idea where this relationship is going, and I don't want to jinx anything.

"Fine," she concedes. "I'll keep my mouth shut about looking like the real deal. But what are you going to tell everyone?"

"Um...that we're friends?"

She scowls again. "You're going back in the closet?"

"No!" I cry, offended, but she's not done.

"You're putting those boys back in the closet as well, you realize."

"No one is getting in any closets," I grumble.

She shakes her head. "But don't you see? If you hide your relationship, that's exactly what you're doing."

I chew on my lip, not wanting to admit she might be right, but also not feeling ready to label what we have just yet. It's all so fragile. Everything in me is screaming to protect those boys, especially our baby, Coco. He's been through so much.

"Colby's family is homophobic," I tell her, looking in the direction they left in. "They tried conversion therapy. I think they hurt him. They definitely disowned them."

When I turn back, Anisha's expression is murderous. "How much does a ticket to Australia cost again?" she snarls.

I laugh at her dramatics, and eventually, she huffs and smiles.

"Fuck them," I say, meaning it. "They don't matter. But I really don't want to hurt Colby in any way or put him in a position of being judged or ostracized by anyone here."

My big sister wraps her arms around me like she used to when I skinned my knee or got bullied at school. But then she leans back to look me in the eye.

"What do you think is going to hurt more, hun? Someone here hypothetically getting weird…or you not wanting to publicly claim this relationship for what it really is in front of your family."

Well…shit.

"I didn't think of it like that," I said heavily.

She hums. "I know you're probably wary of announcing something in its infancy, but you've got to trust me on this one. Grab that happiness when you can. Sometimes life doesn't go the way you'd planned. You don't want to regret anything. Gregory might have turned into a total shit stain in the end, but he wasn't always like that. He used to be fun. He made me smile. I don't regret that or the two awesome daughters he gave me."

I puff out my cheeks and nod at her. "Okay. I'm listening. I'm not saying I'm going to walk in there and announce that

I've gone all woke and got myself two boyfriends just to spite the conservatives, but I promise I'll think about it."

She snorts. "I dunno, that would be pretty hilarious."

"It would," I agree. "I'll talk to my boys about it first, though. I'll definitely tell Mum and Dad before our trip is over."

She's got that devilish sparkle in her eyes again. "You call them 'my boys' a lot. Are you Daddy?"

"W-what?" I splutter. "I…uh…shut up."

She howls with laughter, already dancing her way toward the kitchen. "Don't worry. Your secret's safe with me, Daddy Cool."

I sigh, but a part of me feels better for our talk. I'm still conflicted. But she's right. I'd never, *ever* want my boys to think I was ashamed or embarrassed by them.

I know it's very early days. We've already established that.

But I think I might love them the way they love each other.

They really are my everything.

CHAPTER 21

Colby

Is this what a family is supposed to be like?

I'm genuinely not sure. I used to see families on TV and wonder, but that doesn't seem to do justice to the cacophony going on around me right now. There have to be two dozen people in this house, and they're all eating and laughing and singing and talking.

They're talking to me.

Andreas's relatives want to know who I know him and what I do for a living and how it is living in Sydney and…not in a judgy way. They're just sincerely curious. They listen when I speak and ask follow-up questions. I've had more than one middle-aged lady tell me I'm adorable, and several people have commented that they love my accent.

The thing that really gets me, though, is that these people aren't simply talking to me because I'm next to Jalen and they feel obliged. I lost him some time after we had our proper Christmas dinner, when we were all spread across three large tables. I have no idea how Yuen managed to feed us all, but I think he enlisted the help of some of his and Tianna's siblings to help.

I'd found myself seated between Jalen and Andreas, which was a relief, but we were also lucky enough to have Andreas's grandma, Zhen, opposite us. The more gin she had, the funnier she became.

"You boyfriends!" she yelled more than once, cackling with her paper party hat askew as she pointed across the table at us. I was afraid of what the people around us might think, but they just chuckled along with her, and Andreas didn't deny it.

That in itself was kind of incredible.

I understand that he probably doesn't want to tell his family that we're an official thing as of last night. It's a bit complicated. But the fact that he didn't correct her was somehow good enough for me.

It certainly wasn't a rejection, so I'll take the win for now.

After we'd been stuffed with food, several board games appeared, along with more drinks. There's music being played in every room though some sort of speaker system. Now it's been turned up, and the conversations have gotten louder to match.

River, the dog, has mostly stayed by the fire, lifting her head and wagging her tail when people come to greet her. She's also been acting as a jungle gym for Donna, the English sheepdog puppy that Yuen surprised Tianna with this morning as her Christmas present. Donna has enough energy for five dogs, I'm sure. But River seems to be tolerating her presence well enough.

Zhen has appointed herself as my unofficial protector by looping her arm through mine instead of using her walking cane, then dragging me from table to table to introduce me to relative after relative. Donna follows us, winding around our feet and doing her best to trip us up.

"This Colby! He a writer!" Zhen keeps announcing. I think she got the idea from Jalen. After the third time, I stop trying to correct her. When people ask what kind of books, I tell them it's romance. For a little while, I can make believe that what I'm saying is real.

It feels amazing.

What would it be like to live in a world where I was dating both Jalen and Andreas and instead of dragging myself to a miserable retail job, I spent my days writing fanfiction? Or…maybe even *original books.* That would be so incredible I can't even really picture it. But after a couple of mimosas, my worries fade away, and I decide that it's okay to pretend just for a little while. It's not hurting anyone, after all.

"You a good boy," Zhen says as we take a break and sit on a sofa in the conservatory, where it's a little quieter.

I look over at her as she smiles at me, thinking of my own grandparents back home. My mum's mum is the biggest zealot of the lot and has hit me with her Bible more times than she's ever hugged me. I lost count of how many times she told me I was a sinner.

I'm pretty sure she never called me 'good.'

"Thank you, Zhen," I say thickly.

She shakes her head. "You call me Nai Nai. You a good boy. You good for my Andy."

Tears sting my eyes, but I smile back at her. "He's very good for me as well."

She jabs her elbow into my ribs. "Handsome, too, no?"

I drop my head back and laugh. It feels *so* good. I'm not walking on eggshells or afraid that I'll be screamed at once everyone's gone home. I feel free. Accepted. Authentic.

And brave, like Buckets. I'm managing this party by myself. I hope Jalen isn't worrying about me, even though I'm certain he is, as that's been his job for years. But I'm doing okay, especially with my bodyguard by my side.

"Would you like another drink, Nai Nai?" I ask. "Maybe a cup of tea."

She frowns at me. "More gin," she says like I'm trying to swindle her out of a refill.

I grin and take her glass. "Coming right up."

The kitchen is empty, as I assume everyone else is spread over the living and dining rooms, engaged in one of the several games going on. Donna follows me there, sniffing frantically all over the floor. I'm sure she's searching for every crumb that's been dropped there, but I don't think a few little scraps will hurt her, so I let her forage.

I'm just rummaging through the bottle collection for the gin when I hear a raised voice coming from the entrance hall. I barely catch it over the music and all the voices, but I'm so incredibly attuned to even the first hint of an argument I know not to second guess when the hairs on the back of my neck rise.

I look around, but there's no one else I think could have heard. It's not my house and it's not my family, so my first instinct is to just grab my drinks, head back to the conservatory, and pretend like nothing ever happened.

But then I catch just a snatch of a word, and I realize I recognize that voice.

It's Andreas's youngest niece, Isla.

And she's upset.

Before I even know what my feet are doing, I'm walking quickly out of the kitchen toward the front door, Donna right by my side. The air is cold because Isla is holding it open, and on the other side is a grown man. The way he's clinging to the doorframe suggests he's been at the gin a lot harder than Nai Nai. But it's the way he's looming over the little girl that spikes fear into my heart.

"Dad, Mum already said," Isla hisses anxiously. "You need to go! You're supposed to pick us up tomorrow!"

"Isla?" I call out as I get closer. She turns around, and when she sees me, her shoulders visibly sag in relief.

"Colby!"

But that also draws the man's attention to me, and I don't like the way his eyes narrow one bit. Gregory. I'm sure that's what Andreas said his ex-brother-in-law was called. He's good-looking in a classically handsome way, I suppose. He's wearing an expensive-looking suit, and the watch on his wrist looks very fancy. But the way he curls his lip at me is anything but attractive.

"Oh, so this is one of them, is it?"

My blood runs cold. He knows who I am? What does he mean by that?

"Dad, *stop* it," Isla snaps. "You shouldn't be snooping on my Instagram anyway."

Her comment doesn't make sense for a second until I remember that earlier she and her sister asked Jalen and me to take a photo together with a progress Pride flag they'd brought with them from home. They said they wanted to tell their mates about their uncle's 'cool new friends.'

I stupidly thought they meant in a private chat.

But what do I care if they made public posts? They're very enthusiastic allies in ways that make me think they might be queer in some way they're not even aware of yet. Or maybe they're just sweet, open-minded girls. Either way, that's not the problem. I'm proud to be out now that I've escaped my family.

However, the drunk guy currently sneering at me looks like he could be a problem. A big one.

"Isla," I say uncertainly, addressing her rather than her dad. "Do you want me to get your mum?"

"Her *mum* is the whole bloody problem," Gregory cries, stumbling over the threshold. Isla gasps and jumps back closer to me. But then she folds her arms and scowls as Donna yelps and growls by my ankles.

"I hate it when you're like this," Isla spits out. Goodness me. She's about a hundred times braver than I've ever been with my own relatives and I'm over twice her age.

"That woman shouldn't be exposing you to these sorts of perverts," Gregory says, jabbing his finger at me.

I freeze. I can't breathe. It's like I'm right back in that awful church with all those terrible people yelling at me that I had to 'pray the gay away' or I was going straight to hell.

"Dad!" Isla yells.

"I-I'm not…" I manage to utter.

Gregory scoffs and flicks his suit jacket back to put his hands on his hips. "I never liked her brother. I always told her to keep him away from you, princess. He was bad enough. But now he's a fucking pedo dating little boys. You *stay away* from my girls!"

He lunges forward a step, making me flinch and poor Isla scream as she throws her arms around my waist. Donna really starts barking now.

"Dad!" Isla shrieks. "I'm serious! Stop it! Colby is lovely, and you shouldn't say such awful things about him."

He gives her a simpering smile that makes me feel sick. "Princess, he's a bad man. You need to get away from him this instant."

"This is why I never want to go round your house," Isla shouts back. "I don't care what some stupid judge said. You're mean!"

She's crying, and I can't say I blame her. I hug her to my side. I'm shaking so badly and my throat is clamped up, but I can at least comfort her like that. Donna barks again, making Gregory wince.

"Can't you *shut* that thing up? Look, princess," he tries again, but then a slim young woman in a skin-tight, plunging red dress appears behind him, shivering with her arms folded.

"Greg, what are you doing?" she demands. "The taxi wants to know how much longer he has to wait, and so do I."

"I'm just getting my girls," Gregory says through gritted teeth. The woman rolls her eyes, and Isla hugs me tighter. "Come on, princess. Go get your sister and your things. It's not safe for you here."

"Stop calling me princess!" Isla yells.

The woman huffs and glares at Isla. "She doesn't want to come, Greg. We were supposed to pick them up tomorrow anyway. Let's just go to the party. Come on."

"Not without my—" Gregory starts.

But he doesn't get to finish.

"YOU!" a voice bellows from behind me. I turn to see Nai Nai struggling down the hallway with fire in her eyes and her finger pointed like a loaded gun.

I run to her side to help her walk, but she seems to be powered by pure fury as she storms toward Gregory by the front door.

"You not welcome. Out, OUT!"

"Oh, come back when you finally speak English, old woman," Gregory slurs with an eye roll. "This little nonce doesn't need some granny protecting him." He tilts his head. "Actually, maybe he does. He looks like a stiff breeze would knock him over."

I want to curl up and die. I can't bear that I'm causing a scene in Andreas's family home when they've all been so welcoming to me. "I'm so sorry," I whisper.

Isla's head snaps toward me, her tears vanishing in an instant. "Don't you dare apologize! Dad, just take Heather and go, all right?"

The young woman—Heather, I assume—has already wandered outside, clearly fed up with the conversation, the barking, and not to mention she's probably freezing her arse off.

"You a bad, terrible, ugly man," Nai Nai spits out. "You leave lovely Colby alone. He a good boy."

I stare at her, unable to believe how she's defending me. And Isla, too. I don't deserve this.

"Hey, what's going on out here?" a new voice calls from behind. Tianna. "Gregory? We weren't expecting you until tomorrow."

"I'm sorry, Nana," Isla cries. "He saw my Insta. Then he called me saying he was outside and I had to let him in. He's saying awful things about Uncle Andy and Colby and Jalen."

Tianna's face turns to thunder. But behind her, several more people have materialized in time to hear Isla's words.

Including Andreas and Jalen.

"Baby?" Jalen says as he runs to my side and throws his arms around me. He's wearing a thigh-length skirt over some thick tights, and I don't miss the way Gregory's eyes bug out of his head. "Are you okay?"

"I'm fine. I—"

"You!" Gregory barks, this time jabbing his finger at Andreas. "I never fucking liked you, and now you're bringing your pervy, underage boyfriends around my daughters? You should all be arrested!"

"They older than your child bride," Nai Nai grumbles. "Much more pretty, too."

"Gregory," Anisha snaps. "If you want to see your daughters at all this Christmas, I suggest you shut up, leave, and go get sober."

Isla runs over to her and Esme. "I don't want to go to his place tomorrow, Mum. Please don't make us. He's so homophobic."

"The custody agreement says—" Gregory begins.

"That agreement doesn't mean shit if my girls don't feel safe with you," Anisha fires back.

Gregory sways on the spot for a moment before his gaze narrows again, and this time he's got both Jalen and me in his sights.

"This is all *your* fault!" he shouts. When he lunges this time, I don't doubt he means to put his hands on us.

And he probably would have. If in that split second, Andreas didn't appear in front of us like a human shield.

"Touch my boyfriends, and I'll put you on your arse," he growls. Donna runs around his legs, barking nonstop. Even River has risen from her place by the fire to come sit by Andreas's side, and manages a deep *woof* of support.

The fear of being hit again after all this time almost made me black out. I think I'm only still standing because Jalen is holding me up.

But hearing Andreas announce in front of his *entire family* that we're his boyfriends threatens to take my legs out from under me all over again.

Gregory only just manages to stop himself in time to stagger backward. "Pervert," he snarls.

"Says the man who left my sister for a gold-digging teenager," Andreas says calmly.

Tianna steps in front of us to stand side by side with her son, crossing her arms. "Andreas, Colby, and Jalen are all welcome in this house," she says clearly. "You are not. I suggest you don't come back tomorrow. Anisha will contact you in the new year."

"Anisha's *lawyer* will contact you in the new year," she amends from behind us.

"This is my family," Andreas says. He moves to pull me and Jalen into his arms. "*All* of them. If you weren't so full of hate, maybe you'd still be a part of it. I feel sorry for you, Gregory, I really do. I hope that young woman out there sees who you really are before she marries you, and escapes. But really, that's her problem. Now, leave."

The anger has apparently blown out of Gregory, and he looks like he's going to cry. It's pretty revolting. "Nishy, please," he blubbers.

"Out!" Anisha yells.

"Please, leave our home now," Tianna says firmly as Yuen steps forward and ushers Gregory back toward the threshold.

Even both the dogs bark a farewell.

Finally, Gregory snaps and spins on his heels, slamming the door behind him.

"Bye, Felicia," Nai Nai says smugly.

Voices erupt behind us, but Andreas just whips me and Jalen around to hug us to him tightly. "Are you boys okay?" he asks thickly. I realize he's shaking.

"Daddy, I'm fine," I say quietly.

No one's going to hear me over all the commotion behind us. But they might notice when Andreas kisses both Jalen and me on the tops of our heads and crushes us even more with his fiercely protective hug.

"They'll see," I protest weakly.

Andreas's laugh is rueful. "Oh, baby boy. I *want* them to see. I want them to know you're both mine."

"Really?" Jalen asks. For once, he sounds as unsure as I feel.

Andreas turns us all around so we're facing his many, *many* relatives, who are practically climbing the doorframes of the living and dining rooms so they can watch all the drama in the hallway.

"See," Nai Nai says. Someone's fetched her walking stick for her, and she flicks it toward us three. "Boyfriends. I tell you."

Tianna raises her eyebrows, a small smile playing on her lips. "Andy? Is that true?"

I look up at my Daddy as he looks between me and Jalen. "Absolutely," he says proudly.

That causes another ripple of sound, including cheers from Isla and Esme and more barking from Donna. Tianna moves forward, her arms open as she embraces all three of us. I feel a thump and realize that Anisha has also joined in the hug.

"I'm so happy for you all," Tianna says warmly.

"Congrats on doing the right thing," Anisha says proudly. "Sorry about my arsehole ex."

"Language," Tianna tuts, but Anisha just laughs.

I'm so overwhelmed as I cling to Andreas and Jalen. My best friend manages to catch my eye amid all the tangled limbs.

"Are you okay?" he asks me again.

I take a deep breath, feeling the literal love all around me.

To me, family has always been something to be afraid of. I didn't think I was worthy of love. I never thought anyone could possibly care for me because I was broken. Nothing special.

And yet I have Jalen and Andreas, who have been relentless in showing me how much I mean to them. Now Andreas's family threw out someone who'd once been considered a member of this family in order to protect me.

I'm not sure there are enough words to describe how I'm feeling, and I love words.

I try my best, though.

"I'm perfect," I tell my best friend truthfully before looking up at my Daddy. "Everything's perfect."

And when he leans down and kisses me gently on the mouth, I know it's really true.

CHAPTER 22

Andreas

THAT WAS CERTAINLY THE MOST MEMORABLE CHRISTMAS DAY I've ever had. I'm angry at Gregory's extremely unwanted intrusion.

But I can't say I'm mad at how my family behaved in response to it.

My sister's words had already sunk into me from our chat earlier. I didn't want my boys to think I wasn't proud of being with them. But I wanted to wait for the right time to let people know, preferably individually, with as little fuss and fanfare as I could manage.

It turns out that a messy but heartfelt public declaration was also a good way to go.

Nobody had anything negative to say, not even in jest. In fact, after Gregory's disgusting behavior, even if people were surprised or had queries, they certainly didn't come to me. I imagine they were polite enough to wait until we left before grilling my immediate family some more on the matter.

I trusted that Anisha and the girls would probably be able to field any questions any of our less-informed relatives might have. I am far more interested in taking my boys back home for the night and showing them *exactly* how much they are mine.

It takes a while to say goodbye as everybody wants a hug and to ask if we're okay. I tell them all to go fuss over Isla instead, who was the one who stood up to her awful father all by herself to begin with.

I couldn't believe it at first when I found out that Colby came to her rescue. But then I know it to be true with my whole heart. My baby boy is braver than he thinks.

It's harder to separate the boys from Donna and River, especially when Donna is determined to make a jailbreak and sneak outside with us. The boys obviously adore both the girls and I'm really glad to see that they love dogs as much as I do. I've toyed with getting one back home in Sydney, but I worried it wasn't fair, as I lived alone and worked so much.

Maybe that won't be such a problem anymore? Something to consider for the new year.

Eventually, we manage to make our escape, and I order an Uber as we put our coats, shoes, and accessories on. It's a good thing I insisted on the boys packing hats, gloves, and scarves for traveling home that night.

Because when we step outside, it's snowing.

"No way!" Jalen shrieks, immediately spinning around and opening his mouth to catch flakes on his tongue. "It's a white Christmas!"

I shake my head in disbelief. "Well, I never," I say. "That really is a Christmas miracle."

Colby slips his hand against mine and bites his lip as he smiles. "We're the miracle," he says sweetly. "Us three."

I lean down and kiss his cold lips. "Damn straight, baby Coco," I agree. "Come on, firecracker!" I yell after Jalen, who is currently running around between the parked cars with his arms out, pretending to be an angel. "Let's go home. We can play in the snow tomorrow when it's settled."

"You promise?" he asks breathlessly as he jogs back up to us. We walk down the driveway together.

"Cross my heart," I say.

I'll never lie to these boys for as long as I live, not if I can help it.

I low-key hate sitting up in front of the Uber when all I want to do is keep my arms wrapped around my boys. But we're not in the car long and I remind myself that there's no rush.

We have all the time in the world now.

When we get back to the house, the snow is still falling. I think of that Taylor Swift song and wonder if it's settling on the beach. We can look tomorrow. I love the idea of having snowball fights and making snow angels with my boys, but knowing the British weather, we'll probably only get a small flurry tonight, and it'll have melted by morning.

Ah, well. It's still magical now, especially after how many times I told the boys it definitely wouldn't snow and that we'd probably just get rained on the whole time. It's like the universe is rewarding me for getting my act together and finally visiting my family.

The holiday rental has a smart thermostat, so I was able to crank the heating up via my phone before we even left my parents' place. It's toasty warm as we step inside and start peeling off our outdoor wear in a hurry.

It'll feel even better once we're naked.

Before Jalen can run up the stairs, I grab his wrist and spin him around to capture his mouth for a kiss. Colby slips his hand into my free one before I even pull away, ready for me to kiss him next.

"Are we going to your bedroom?" Jalen asks hopefully with a giggle, but I shake my head.

Before he can get too disappointed, I elaborate.

"It's *our* bedroom for the rest of the trip," I say, a hungry growl underlying my words.

His eyes get wide as he looks between me and Colby. Then he grins and grabs Colby's hand. "Race you there!" he cries as the two boys charge up the stairs.

I laugh and jog after them, not sad at watching their cute bums bouncing all the way out of sight onto the landing.

I know what I want from them tonight. Now it's just a case of seeing if that's what they'd enjoy, too.

My skin is tingling and my cock throbbing by the time I make it to the bedroom. But my pulse skyrockets when I discover the two of them giggling, kissing, and hastily stripping each other's clothes off. I arrive just in time to see Jalen yank down Colby's jeans and underwear before whipping off the sparkly skirt and tights he's been wearing all day. They're naked and perfect and mine.

"Daddy's turn!" he announces as he and Colby rush for me, pulling off my jumper, turning it inside out as it drops to the floor. The kisses are messy, and the hands are frantic as we finally tumble onto the bed. My heart is pounding, and my head is dizzy with lust.

I want to do *everything.* But I remind myself again that there's no rush.

Who knows how many nights we're going to get the chance to spend together?

Maybe all of them.

"Hang on a second, sweet boys."

I sit on my knees and pull them up to do the same so we're facing each other in a little triangle. I want to be serious, but it's a bit difficult with three hard dicks standing to attention between us. So I grin and shake my head before cupping a hand against each of my boys' faces.

"Is everything okay?" Colby asks sweetly.

"Everything's wonderful," I assure him. "I just wanted to touch base with what we'd like to do tonight."

"What do *you* want to do, Daddy?" Jalen asks, his eyes sparkling as he bounces on his heels. I know he's aware that's making his cock waggle temptingly at me, so I narrow my eyes at him, determined to get everyone's consent in line before we get on with the fun stuff.

"Naughty boy," I grumble. "I was hoping we might use your presents, actually."

He frowns in thought for a second before glancing over at the bedside table. "The condoms?" he asks excitedly.

I nod and consider my words for a second. "I was thinking we could maybe use two of them?"

My boys' eyes go wide. However, I focus on Colby first.

"How would you feel, baby Coco, if Jay Jay made love to you and I made love to him at the same time?"

He gasps and glances at Jalen, who looks like his brain might be short-circuiting. I hope in a good way.

"Really?"

I nod. "If you lie on your back, we can both watch you while we do."

At that, he blushes furiously and ducks his head like he's trying to hide. That's exactly why I want to do this, though. I want him to be seen as he comes undone. I want him to understand that he's loved when he's at his most vulnerable.

We're going to have many firsts together as a throuple, I'm sure. But I know that the first time we go all the way that I want for Jalen to be the one to be inside him. Their love has crossed oceans for years. They deserve to be as close as they can possibly be tonight.

He's breathing heavily, and his eyes are tearful as he looks back at me. I notice that Jalen is unusually quiet as he waits for his best friend to respond, which seems so respectful to me. I know he's my noisy little firecracker, but he's also thoughtful and tender as well.

"Um, yes, please," Colby mumbles, still struggling to look me in the eyes. But a tiny smile plays on his lips, and his cock jerks excitedly at the thought of us claiming him like that. I don't blame him. My blood is racing just thinking about it.

"Yesss," Jalen says in a quiet celebration. I love that he wants to show his enthusiasm without spooking Colby too much. "Can I make a suggestion, Daddy?"

I lean over and kiss his neck, making him shiver. "Of course, Jay Jay."

He doesn't say anything, so I laugh and remove my lips from his skin to give his big brain a chance to function.

"Oh, um," he says with a dazed giggle. "I thought you could finger me while you watch me rim Colby so we're both nice and stretched."

Colby chokes on nothing, his eyes bugging out of his head. I laugh at him, but not unkindly.

"I think you're going to have to get used to our little firecracker's filthy mouth, baby boy."

Jalen nods sagely. "You really are because I have, like, a whole laundry list of completely despicable things I want to do to you. And that's *nothing* to the debauchery I want Daddy to unleash on me."

"Oh," Colby squeaks, biting his lip as he looks between us, a laugh bubbling up his throat. "Okay, then. I better, um, start getting used to it right now, then."

"Yay!" Jalen says, clapping his hands and bouncing on the mattress. "Lie on your tummy, please. I want to taste you. Oh! Have you ever done this before?"

Colby gulps. "N-no," he admits.

Jalen leans in to gently kiss his mouth. "I'm going to treat you like a queen, baby boy. Don't you worry. It's going to feel amazing, I promise."

Colby nods. "I trust you. I trust you both."

I kiss him then, placing my hand against his chest and feeling his heart beating like a hummingbird's wings. "Thank you, sweetheart. We'll always do everything to earn that trust, that's my promise. If you don't like something or you need a break, you just say stop. Understood?"

"Yes, Daddy," he says earnestly.

I don't think I'm ever going to get tired of being called that. I get shivers up my spine every single time.

Jalen helps Colby lie on his front with his head on a pillow, then spreads his legs and starts kissing up his thighs. It's doubtful that I'm ever going to need the help of the internet again to get horny, not when I have the two most beautiful boys who want to pleasure each other so desperately.

I bite my lip as Jalen begins licking Colby's tight bud, pulling his cheeks apart so he can show me every gorgeous touch. His hole is soon glistening and fluttering as Colby whimpers and mewls into the pillow.

The temptation to just wank off watching that is strong. But I know what's to come will be even better.

Especially when Jalen already has his pert arse in the air, inviting me to take advantage of it.

I don't really want to tear my eyes away from the delicious sight of one of my boys eating out the other, but I have to in order to grab the lube and condoms from the side cabinet. I'm back in a flash, though, dropping the two condoms by my knee and squeezing lube onto my fingers.

"This will be a little cold," I warn Jalen, nuzzling my lips against the shell of his ear before nipping at his lobe. He gasps as I start rubbing my slicked-up fingers against his entrance, but then he's humming again as he works Colby's hole, kissing, sucking, and pushing his tongue inside.

I lean back so I'm upright on my knees, drinking in the

sight of my fingers disappearing inside Jalen as he pleasures Colby's most intimate area. The bedroom is warm, and we're all dripping with perspiration already, filling the air with our delicious musky scent. Colby is still whimpering and writhing on the mattress. My fingers as well as Jalen's lips make erotic squelching noises.

Jalen pulls back and kisses Colby's cheek before wiping his mouth, then looking behind him. He reaches for the bottle of lube, so I hand it to him wordlessly. He drizzles some onto his fingers, then gently eases two inside our sweet boy, making him wail.

"That's it, baby Coco," he says soothingly. His words are strained, presumably from the two fingers I also have inside him, but his tone only shows concern for Colby. "You're doing so well. You look beautiful. Do you think you feel ready for me?"

Colby turns his head to look over his shoulder, blinking woozily at us. "Uh, yeah. I think so. Love you, Jay Jay. Love you, Daddy."

"Aww," Jalen coos with such heartfelt emotion I feel it physically in my chest. "We love you too, boo-boo."

I don't correct him.

Because I'm pretty sure it's true.

He leans forward to kiss Colby's mouth, so I naturally let my fingers slip out and take the opportunity to suit up. My cock is still rock hard after watching all the fun so far, and it's more than ready to see just how good Jalen feels wrapped around it.

First, though, it's Colby's turn. Jalen helps him move onto his back, then gets him to hug his knees to his shoulders. Then he slides a pillow under his lower back to enable him to get a better angle. When he turns to look for his own condom, he finds me ready and waiting to roll it down his shaft.

He clings to my arms as I do, his eyes fluttering shut as he moans. "Thank you, Daddy," he whispers.

"You're welcome, little firecracker," I tell him back, sneaking a quick kiss on his lips, which taste like Colby.

As Jalen lines himself up with Colby's entrance, I trail my fingers up and down Jalen's flanks, loving the feel of his lithe body under my hands. He always calls himself too skinny or too tall, and I've decided that's not going to be allowed anymore because what he is, is perfect. I like that he's different from Colby, who's shorter with a cute, rounded tummy, or my stocky frame. Our differences are what make us beautiful.

Colby bites his lip as sweat runs down his body. He mostly keeps his eyes on Jalen as he pushes farther inside him, but occasionally, his gaze flicks to me. I reach down with one hand and entwine his fingers with mine, so we keep his knee up together.

"Good boy," I murmur.

Both of them groan as Jalen bottoms out, and while he settles, I waste no time in positioning myself behind my little firecracker with my free hand so I can ease my way inside.

He grunts as the head of my throbbing cock pushes its way past his tight ring. I kiss his shoulder and squeeze his hips. "That's it, good boy. You feel so amazing."

"Taylor on a tractor," he utters, making me laugh, and I kiss him again. I'm not a fan of super serious sex. I much prefer it when everyone has fun.

Now that I have my two boys to play with, I'm sure it always will be.

His hot channel sucks me in, feeling as incredible as he and Colby look. Jalen leans down to kiss Colby's mouth, giving me time to fill Jalen up to the hilt.

Then I begin to thrust.

That urges Jalen to move, and both boys wail, filling the

room with their gorgeous sounds of pleasure. I can tell I've found Jalen's prostate, as he's emitting a high pitched squeal and his entire body is shaking.

I love how he's relaxed against me, essentially allowing me to become the driving force not only into him but for his movement into Colby. It makes me feel as if I'm taking them both at once. I squeeze Colby's hand harder, then take my hand from Jalen's hip to wrap my arm around his chest. He drops his head back and rubs his temple against mine as we both gaze down at Colby. His skin is flushed and his breathing frantic as all three of us chase our climaxes.

"Do you want to touch little Coco?" I murmur into Jalen's ear. "I think he'd like you to help him come."

Jalen nods as I continue to piston into him, working both my boys at the same time. He wraps his long fingers around Colby's red and leaking shaft. As soon as he begins stroking it, Colby screams.

"That's it, sweetheart," I encourage him. "Come for Daddy. I want to see you both come."

After a few more moments of frenzied pounding, Colby gnashes his teeth as he starts coming all over his stomach and Jalen's hand. The beautiful sight makes me thrust even more aggressively, loving it when Jalen convulses and screams as well.

It only takes another couple of seconds before I screw up my eyes and let go, bellowing as I blow my load deep inside my sassy boy.

We need a minute for us all to catch our breath. Then it's my job to carefully pull us apart, dispose of the condoms, then fetch a warm, damp flannel from the bathroom to clean us up. I'm grateful that this time I don't need to wash the sheets, but I would have done it gladly if I had to.

Anything for these boys.

I'll need to think about teeth brushing and pajamas in a

minute. We'll have to move to get under the covers at the very least, so we don't wake up shivering at three in the morning.

But just for now, I pull my boys to me and cuddle them tight, pressing gentle kisses on their cheeks and the tops of their heads.

"Merry Christmas, babies."

"Merry Christmas, Daddy," they mumble back.

I have no idea how many Christmases I'll be fortunate enough to have in my lifetime. However, I know without a doubt that none of them will ever be as precious to me as this one has been.

CHAPTER 23

Jalen

THE NEXT FEW DAYS GO PAST IN A BIT OF A HAPPY BLUR. ON Boxing Day, we wake up to a winter wonderland because the snow not only continued to fall but it also settled over several inches. We make the most of it in our yard as well as on the beach, creating snow people and having snowball fights. It's quite an incredible sight to behold, especially having spent almost my entire life in sunny California and then moving to Sydney just as it was getting hot for summer.

We see Andreas's family almost every day, and they're very nice to us, especially Colby, which is the way it should be. This girl can always take care of herself, but Colby is always going to need a lot more assurances that he's welcome and wanted.

Andreas's family do a great job of that.

A couple of days before our flight back to Sydney, we head back to London so we can spend some time sightseeing in the city. I'm sad to say goodbye to our gorgeous holiday rental, Brighton Beach, Andreas's family, and especially River and Donna. But Andreas has booked us a suite in a fancy hotel, and I feel like an actual queen, or at the very least, Julia Roberts in Pretty Woman.

We cram in a lot of tourist stuff, including going up The Shard, the tallest building in all of the UK, watching the Changing of the Guard outside Buckingham Palace, and taking a horse-drawn carriage ride around Richmond Park, drinking mulled wine and eating mince pies. I feel like I'm in Bridgerton.

We also shop till we drop, with Andreas buying us everything we want, from tacky trinkets to designer clothes. I fret about fitting it all in our luggage until Andreas simply buys us another suitcase in order to get it all home.

Our last day is spent in Greenwich as there's loads to do there. They have a market that's half delicious, international food and half handmade crafty goods. There's also the impressive naval college that's been used as a location in several movies and TV shows, and the observatory that sits on top of a hill with a stunning view of the city. I find out that's where time 'starts' and that's why it's called Greenwich Mean Time and not British Standard Time or whatever.

I'm really enjoying myself, so much. But there's something about standing on that hill, looking down over the expansive park that leads to the college with the rest of London as its backdrop, and I feel…small. Helpless.

Because time is the one thing I'm running out of.

And I don't just mean here in England. All vacations come to an end, and even though it's normal to get a bit sad, it's natural. Usually, I look forward to going home again and getting back to my regular everyday life.

I should be even more excited because my everyday life now includes not one but *two* boyfriends, one of whom is the person I've been in love with for what feels like forever.

But the new year is approaching and, with it, my doom.

Why—*why*—did I wait so long to move out to Australia? I

know I had to save up the money and work out the logistics. And to be fair, I had to give Colby a long time to work up to the idea so he wouldn't freak out because me moving continents for him was pretty overwhelming for someone who used to think he was unlovable.

Besides, me moving earlier wouldn't mean we'd have met Andreas any sooner. In fact, your girl has seen Sliding Doors and knows that any one little change could have meant that Colby and I never ended up bidding on the Jurassic Galaxy set at the same time, and therefore we never would have met Andreas at all.

That makes me shiver. Hell to the no, mama!

However, knowing all this doesn't change the fact that I'm going to turn thirty next year, and that means I can't apply for another working holiday visa.

Come July, I'll have to move back to California.

I try my best not to think about it as we walk back down the hill, watching all the dogs running around who are making the most of what's left of the snow. But as our flight from Heathrow looms tomorrow, I can't seem to stop myself.

I'm not exaggerating when I say I don't want to live without Colby and Andreas. The thought of being on the other side of the world to them is inconceivable. My departure date is six months away, but having any date at all makes me feel like I'm living on borrowed time.

How can I enjoy this incredible, sensational, hot AF new relationship when I know it can never last? I don't want it to end. But I don't know how I can stay in Australia, though.

Perhaps I'll have to step aside and let Colby and Andreas be together, after all. That's a small comfort, I guess. I suppose it is a kind of silver lining that they'll have each other.

Before this trip and us getting together, me leaving felt like a distant problem that I wouldn't have to think about for ages. But as we wind down our last evening in London with a delicious dinner at the fancy hotel and a night of passionate love-making, I find the issue has become my constant companion. I feel dimmer. Quieter.

The tighter I try to hold on to these amazing men, the faster I feel them slipping away.

I spend the tube journey to the airport realizing I have to make a decision. I don't want to, but this is what Colby does to me. I knew I wasn't responsible enough to ever be his Daddy. However, he does force me to do what's best for him. I can be responsible if I have to.

So do I squeeze every last drop I can from this amazing, once-in-a-lifetime,   makes-me-want-to-sing-like-a-Disney-princess relationship?

Or do I walk away now and try and break my heart a little less than further down the line?

What would I even do, though? Move out of the flat? Encourage Colby to move in with Andreas and then get myself some random person in as a new roommate? Neither of those options fill me with anything but dread.

However, the more time I spend envisioning having to wave goodbye in July to the two men I love as I walk through the departure gate at Sydney International Airport, the more desolate I become.

Yeah, yeah. I said what I said, even if it's only in my head. I LOVE Andreas. I don't care that it's only been a month. And I know it's a different kind of love than I have for Colby, but he's a different kind of man.

Realizing this is how I feel only twists the knife in my heart harder. So I do the very responsible, mature, adult thing and get absolutely hammered on the flight, crying as I watch several romcoms until we switch planes and I can mercifully spend the last several hours of the journey in a thought-free coma. My dreams might be screwed up, but they're abstract. The pain is dulled, at least for a while.

If Andreas and Colby notice my melancholy, they don't say anything. They just tease me about my hangover once we land in Sydney, but even then, Colby still hugs me, and Andreas picks up my suitcase without a word.

Our body clocks are fucked, so Andreas takes us to the taxi stand so we can get a cab home and probably sleep for the next eighteen hours. Tomorrow is New Year's Eve, so we just need to be recovered in time to get to Andreas's apartment by about eight o'clock so the three of us can spend the night celebrating midnight together.

I'm not sure I'll feel like celebrating, though.

As I throw my clothes off and crawl into my bed, I send a prayer up to the goddesses watching over me that my stupid mood will go away tomorrow so I can at least have fun with my boyfriends while we're all still in the same country.

Sometime during my fitful sleep marathon, I realize that Colby crawls into bed with me. I don't exactly wake up, but I cling to him for dear life.

Somehow I'll work this out. Stupid international laws can't keep us apart. Romance has to overcome them because if anyone deserves a happy ending, it's Colby Wilson.

For now, I let sleep drag me under. With my baby boy wrapped in my arms, things don't seem quite as bad. Who knows what the new year will bring? After the last incredible month we've had, I've got to cling to hope. We have no idea what's about to come around the corner.

I can't give up.

Even if I have no idea how to stop this from happening.

CHAPTER 24

Andreas

I'M USED TO WORRYING ABOUT COLBY.

Jalen is a whole different matter.

I got more and more concerned about him on the journey back from England, but he clearly wasn't going to tell me what was wrong. I didn't want to spoil the end of our trip, and I knew he was going to be jet lagged as all hell, so I didn't push it at the time.

Instead, I focused on fighting off my jet lag by unpacking and then while the day away working on my apartment so it would be ready to host my boys for New Year's. I know they've been here plenty of times by now, but things are different now. They're officially my boyfriends.

I want this celebration to be special for them because they're special. The most special things to me in this whole, wide world.

Whatever is troubling my little firecracker, I'll fix it. We'll work it out together. I just need to find out what it is first.

After New Year's, though. Tonight, I just want to have fun, and watch the fireworks over the Opera House from my balcony with my boys. So I spend the afternoon stringing up fairy lights outside and printing out photos to put in my handmade frame from Jalen, capturing so many memories from our trip to the UK.

I video call with my sister and say hello to our parents along with my nieces. I'm very glad to hear that Gregory hasn't been any more trouble since Christmas Day, and I secretly hope that the girls never have to see him again if they don't want to. I wish everyone a happy new year now, as from experience, I know it'll be impossible to try and get a decent connection later.

Somehow, I manage a trip to the supermarket and say a silent prayer that they're not sold out of everything I want in order to cater for my boys. Even though it won't be as good as my dad's, I do my best to make a curry as well as put together a bunch of nibbles to keep us going until the clock strikes twelve and beyond.

Around six, I feel myself flagging, so I jump into the shower to freshen up, picking out a nice shirt to wear with my favorite jeans. It's silly, but I almost feel a little nervous waiting for them to arrive. This is the longest we've been apart since the day before our flight to England. Logically, I know that in the past eighteen hours, they probably haven't decided they want to break up. Still, when my doorbell rings, my heart leaps in my chest, and I can't stop myself from grinning as I rush across the apartment.

"Happy New Year!" they both cry as soon as I swing open the door. As soon as I see them, everything feels right with the world again.

"Happy New Year," I say warmly as I draw them both into a hug.

Colby looks dapper in a nice polo shirt and jeans, but Jalen has gone all out with a dark, glittering maxi dress, sparkling sandals, and enormous bejeweled earrings. He's even got a little tiara nestled in his curls.

"You look stunning," I say to them both as I close the door and follow them inside. "What can I get you to drink? As it's New Year's I have a whole crate of Champagne."

"Sold!" Jalen says, pointing to the ceiling and doing a twirl than fans his dress out.

My little firecracker. I really hope his problem was something as simple as being sad to leave the UK. Hopefully, he knows that this is just the beginning and that we're going to have even more of an adventure now that we're back home in Sydney.

I've got a party playlist going over my sound system, and Jalen dances his way out onto the balcony. But Colby follows me to the kitchen, and he's looking troubled.

"Baby boy," I say in concern. "Is something the matter?"

He nibbles on his lip and looks up at me. "Daddy, I think Jalen is hiding how worried he is about his visa."

I blink, taken by surprise. "Uh…what? His visa? I thought he was sponsored by his company and has a couple more years yet."

Colby shakes his head. "He's got a working holiday one, so he's good until July. But he'll be thirty then, so he won't be able to get another one."

My stomach drops. I feel terrible—both that I had no idea and that there's an actual possibility that my little firecracker could be taken away from me so soon.

"That's in six months, though," I say, trying to get all the facts. "Do you think that's really what was bothering him on the journey home?"

I pop the first Champagne bottle and start by mixing it with orange juice. We've got a few hours to go until midnight, after all, and I want us all to remember it.

Colby looks out toward the balcony, where Jalen is dancing by himself. Right now, he looks like he doesn't have a care in the world. "Maybe? He was talking in his sleep last

night, and I definitely heard the words 'visa,' 'home,' and 'no.'"
He frowns. "He also said that Beyoncé was guest starring on
the Eras tour, but I don't think that was really relevant."

I laugh and kiss him on the top of his head. I love the idea
that they slept in the same bed last night. "When are Bay and
Tay *not* relevant?" I ask, having learned from my little firecracker that the answer is 'never.'

But I turn over Colby's words thoughtfully. "If that's
what's on his mind, I'm sure we can work out a solution to
fix it so he can stay in Sydney longer. My work sponsors
visas all the time."

Colby hums and takes a second glass out for Jalen. I hang
back for a second, just watching my boys from afar. The fairy
lights illuminate them against the evening sky, and I almost
want to bottle to the moment forever.

But on the other hand, I don't. I want to keep moving
forward. I'm glad Colby gave me an inkling as to what might
be bothering Jalen, but we've got six months to fix that. I'm
not going to let a silly little detail like that deter me.

Things like international borders won't stand in the way
of true love, not on my watch.

So I head outside and join them in a dance party until
we're all panting and need drink refills. We sit down for
some food, talking and laughing as the clock creeps
through the hours. When we near midnight, I top up our
glasses and put the TV on in the living room so we can
watch the coverage and hear all the people counting down
from ten. The three of us join in on the balcony, yelling the
numbers at the top of our lungs until we hit 'one' then
scream "HAPPY NEW YEAR!" The fireworks erupt both
from across the harbor and on the TV where we can hear
the accompanying music soundtrack. I kiss Colby first,
then Jalen. I lean back, expecting to watch my boys also
kiss.

Instead, Jalen and I discover Colby has gotten down on one knee.

My jaw drops, and Jalen shrieks as he grabs my arm, both of us looking down at Colby in confusion and not a small amount of excitement.

"Boo-boo?" Jalen squeaks.

Colby isn't holding any ring, but he reaches up for Jalen's hand all the same. He's shaking from head to toe and looks as pale as a ghost, but he takes a deep breath and nods to himself before speaking.

"I know you're worrying about having to go home in July," Colby says to Jalen. "But that's okay. You don't have to. There's a really easy solution. Because I've loved you as long as I've known you, Jalen Garcia. That's never, ever going to change. The only thing that's changed is discovering that you feel the same way. So will you please, please marry me, and then you'll never have to leave. We'll be family forever."

He didn't stutter over a single word. I've never been prouder of him in the entire time I've known him. I turn to look at Jalen, seeing the tears streaming down his face.

Somehow his false eyelashes and glitter still remain intact.

"Little Coco, are you sure?" he hiccups.

Colby laughs, tears also falling from his eyes. "I've never been more sure about anything. I'm not just asking to keep you in the country, but that is the best place for you to be if we want to continue having sex."

That barks a laugh from both me and Jalen, and I can't help but marvel at this newly upgraded version of Colby. We're only minutes into the new year, and it already suits him so well.

"In that case, YES!" Jalen screams, dropping to his knees and throwing his arms around Colby. *"Ariana on an airplane! Yes, yes, a billion times, YES!"* He grabs Colby's face and plants a firm kiss on his mouth, transferring a little gloss. When they break apart and look at me, they both look so pretty. "What about Daddy?"

I smile and go down on my knees one at a time, placing a hand on each of their backs. The fireworks are still exploding behind them, and I couldn't imagine a more dazzling scene if I tried.

"What about me?" I ask.

Jalen looks between me and Colby. "Will you marry us, too?"

I laugh and hug them to me. "Not yet, sweetheart."

Jalen pulls back and looks astonished. Colby bites his lip.

"Not *yet,*" I repeat. "It's very soon. Plus, call me a dinosaur, but I always dreamed of being the one to propose to the man I loved. If I'm lucky enough to have *two* men I love, then that requires double the proposal."

"You love us?" Colby asks sweetly.

I laugh again at how he's proved my point. That bit needed to come first in my mind.

"I love you *so much,*" I assure them both, kissing them one after the other. "And someday I'm sure I'll want to marry you as much as the law will let us. But for now, all I care about is keeping our little firecracker firmly by our side. So let's have a wedding."

Jalen holds his finger up at me. "Just a little one," he says sternly. "We'll have a proper one for all three of us, okay?"

I grab his hand and kiss the tip of that finger. "Okay, little firecracker."

He grins before turning back to Colby and shaking his head. "It literally never occurred to me that marriage would fix the visa issue. I can't believe *you* proposed! That's got to be one of the most unbelievable and incredible things that's ever happened in my life!"

Colby nibbles his lip and looks between us. "You make me

brave," he says shyly. "And…honestly, it seemed like the most obvious solution to me."

We all laugh and hug tightly together as the fireworks finally fade. The new year is here. And with it comes a world of possibilities.

I can't wait.

Epilogue

COLBY – TWO YEARS LATER

I look around the beach, and my heart is full. There's nothing like Christmas on the beach, after all.

Especially if both my partners' families are all there with us. Plus our friends. Even our dog, Buckets, is there.

I take a deep breath and look back at my Daddy and my Jay Jay. "Yes," I say with more confidence than I've ever had in my life. "I do."

The officiant beams at the three of us as we all hold hands. "Jalen Garcia. Your union with Colby Wilson is recognized by law. But today, we are here to witness the two of you also joining with Andreas Lau. Do you promise to love both these men, to cherish them in sickness and in health, for as long as you all shall live?"

"Honey, you *know* I do," Jalen says, laughing as he carefully flicks a tear away from his perfectly made-up face. As usual, waterworks aren't enough to budge a lash or any glitter, especially not on such an important day.

We're all wearing white for the ceremony. Andreas has a beautiful suit, I'm a little more casual in slacks and a flowing shirt, and of course Jalen is wearing a sparkly dress. It's a simple halter neck that he's accessorized with a flower crown and a bouquet of white roses.

My beautiful best friend. My handsome Daddy. I feel like my love for them is as big as the ocean itself.

"And finally," the officiant continues. "Do you, Andreas Lau, take Jalen Garcia and Colby Wilson to be your partners in life? To love and to hold, to cherish in sickness and in health, till death do you part?"

Andreas lets out a breath, his eyes shimmering with tears. "I do," he says, squeezing our hands tightly.

After the Christmas when we met, we didn't waste much time. Despite Andreas wanting to hold off proposing, he moved us into his apartment before January was done. Jalen and I had a small ceremony to make our marriage legal, but I'll be honest that didn't make things feel all that different. I was still on such a high from the fact that we'd started dating each other as well as Andreas, that little bit of paper was really just a formality.

A formality that kept Jalen in the country, though. And that meant everything.

I allowed myself to be bullied by both my partners into not going back to a retail job that crushed my soul. For a while, I got a part-time job at the Royal Botanic Garden next to the Opera House. I just did simple things like raking leaves and watering plants. But I enjoyed doing physical labor out in the fresh air. It gave me time to breathe.

And to write.

At first, I just dipped my toe back into fanfiction. I was amazed to realized that a lot of my Jurassic Galaxy followers still had alerts set up for me, and they were thrilled when I became active again. That gave me the courage to start writing original stories. Silly, sci-fi gay love stories, but they brought me so much joy.

Thanks to the unrelenting love and support from my partners, I actually believed they were pretty good.

When Andreas worked out I was serious about maybe trying to self-publish one, he insisted that I quit the gardening and treat writing like a full-time job. He sorted out a proper office space for me, encouraged me to keep steady hours, helped me set up a social media presence, and naturally designed me a logo. A really good one.

My first book came out three months ago, with another one dropping soon and two more in the works.

Sometimes…dreams really do come true.

Thanks to our marriage giving him permanent residency here, Jalen was able to leave the boring office job, instead getting a junior position in an events management company that he's thriving in. One day I can see him putting on major events like televised awards ceremonies or something, but for now, he's helping make corporate Christmas party dreams come true. He gets to glitter and shine every single day, as he should.

Andreas proposed on Christmas Eve last year. It wasn't exactly a surprise, but Jalen and I still both cried our eyes out. What did surprise me was that I thought he'd do something classic and super romantic like a picnic on the beach or at a candle-lit dinner.

Nope.

Jalen and I arrived at the apartment after he'd sent us out grocery shopping. In a few hours, he somehow managed to turn our living room into a replica of the Jurassic Galaxy ship's bridge with custom-printed backdrops, working props, and cutouts of some of the characters. It was so cheesy but at the same time the most incredible, romantic, perfect setting ever.

The best thing, though, was that he *dressed up as Buckets* for when he dropped to one knee, a ring in both hands for each of us. The silver bands had crushed, multicolored gems set in them so they kind of look like sparkling galaxies on our fingers.

It's a matching ring that he now slips on his left hand, and my breath catches as all three of them dazzle in the sunshine.

"I now pronounce you husbands," the officiant declares happily. "You may now kiss each other!"

A cheer rings out from all our family and friends. Nai Nai is front and center, waving her order of service like it's a royal standard and she's charging into battle. Anisha raises her glass of Champagne while Isla and Esme fly the same progressive Pride flag we took photos with two years ago. Tianna and Yuen hold each other as they both shed a tear. Chloe, our flower girl, is currently guarding Jalen's bouquet in her arms as if it's the crown jewels.

Gregory was not invited. In fact, the girls haven't seen him since that day.

I can't believe how many of our family and friends made the epic journey out here to celebrate with us today, our third Christmas Eve together. Now the day has tripled in significance for us. It's the day we got together, the day we got engaged, and now, the day we got married.

It's not lost on me that Jalen's family have come from America, and Andreas's from the UK, Jamaica, and Hong Kong.

Yet my own family lives a couple of hours away, and I didn't even think to invite them.

I wish I had relatives who loved me, but the truth is, I have all the family I could possibly wish for right here with us. The extended Laus and Garcias have effortlessly accepted me as one of their own, and seeing them here today makes me feel more loved than ever.

Buckets the dog barks his approval as we messily kiss each other individually and at the same time—basically any way we can. Then Andreas turns us around with his arms wrapped around my and Jalen's back. The cheering just gets louder, so we take a little bow, laughing the whole time as people take photos of us with our dog on the beach.

It couldn't be more perfect.

I don't think I could feel luckier if I tried. I spent my whole life feeling like I was this disgusting, unlovable thing. Now I have more kinds of love that I know what to do with. Love for my men and their families. Love for my job. Love for our dog and our home, which is soon going to upgrade to a house with a garden…and maybe a nursery? Andreas joked that *Three Men and a Baby* was a movie back in the eighties, but we've talked it over a lot.

One day, when we're a little more settled, the idea of raising a child together feels like it might be the next step for our already perfect family. Maybe more than one.

When I was a teenager, I was told that my future was going to be fire and brimstone. But now I know it's going to be overflowing with happiness and community and hope.

And that all officially starts today, with my two husbands by my side.

———

Thank you so much for reading **Andreas, Jalen, and Colby's** story! If you enjoyed their Christmas adventure, please leave a review on your favorite bookish site. It makes a big difference for us indie authors!

Have you read all the other books in the **A Daddy For Christmas** series? Make sure you don't miss a single one of these delightful stories that readers have been raving about!

https://mybook.to/adaddyforchristmas2023

Turn the page to discover more heartwarming Daddy books by Helen Juliet/HJ Welch.

———

Thank you to my team!
    Cover Design: Jo Clement
    Editing: Meg Cooper
    Proof Reading: Tanja Ongkiehong
    Australian proofers: Patti Mac, Tania Reads, and Myf Wren
    Formatting (and general awesomeness): Ed Davies
    Love and support: Hubby and our cats

BEARS-4-U (MULTI-AUTHOR SHARED UNIVERSE): KEEP ME BY HJ WELCH

Snowed in for a second chance at love...

BECKETT

It's been over two years since I lost my darling husband, and my best friend is taking matters into her own hands. She's signed me up to a dating app for bears and those that love them, even encouraging me to attend a weekend mixer. I go to humor her, not expecting to rescue the most adorable boy...twice. But I'm not ready to open up my heart again, am I?

LAURIE

My last Daddy was bad news. It's taken a lot of courage for me to reach out on Bears-4-U and go to this mixer, only to find that the new Daddy I've been talking to is just as awful. That's when Beckett swoops into my life like a hero in a story book. I know he's not looking for love, but I want to mend his broken heart so badly. When a scary snowstorm blows in and strands us, I trust he'll keep me safe and warm. I want to be in his life, in his bed, in his heart…forever.

Bears-4-U is a MM Daddy romance multi-author series, featuring a host of delicious Daddy pairings. The Bears-4-U dating app is all about putting Bears and Teddy Bears together for their honey-sweet HEAs. Psst, no real bears involved. Each book can be read as a standalone, but why not snuggle up with all the bears?

Click here to get the Keep Me eBook

he can't miss this opportunity, not even when his past comes back to haunt him.

————

Wild Ride

When Red is chased into the woods, he seeks sanctuary at his estranged grandma's house. He doesn't expect to be rescued by his older brother's best friend, the man he was always madly in love with. Could Hunter be the Daddy of Red's wildest dreams? Especially when he unlocks a secret passion of Red's for beautiful lingerie. There's still a threat lurking in the woods, though, and Hunter realises he'll do anything to protect his beautiful boy.

————

Three

When three shy best friends sign up to a dating app to finally get some by the end of the year, they don't expect to all fall for the same gorgeous, slightly scary-looking Daddy. The only solution? Let him choose who he wants to bed. Except he doesn't. Daddy Wolf wants to spoil each little piggy, one after another. But when danger comes calling, will their love for each other be enough to save them all?
Includes Halloween bonus scene!

————

Nine Lives

When Charlie suddenly finds himself homeless and penniless, he decides to sell the only thing left he owns. Himself. For the very first time. Lucky for him he stumbles across Miller, the own of a London kink club, who saves him from those who would take advantage of him. As Miller discovers his inner Daddy, he also unlocks Charlie's kitten alter-ego. But with both their families meddling, will new love be enough to keep them together?

Click here to get the Daddy's Fairy Tales eBook bundle

I've spent almost four years trying to get my captain Seth to notice me. He's hot as hell and knows how to boss a guy around, even one as big as me. To him, though, I'm just the team clown. But when he drags me into this graduation bet, it's no laughing matter. So why shouldn't this little cherub Gabe tutor me as well? In fact, I don't see why we can't share him in all *kinds* of ways. Seth is clearly a natural Daddy, Gabe thrives being doted on, and I'm happy to Daddy *and* be Daddied. Win-win, right?

GABE

Somehow, I've found myself standing up to the guy whose family pretty much owns Paddle Creek and put my neck on the line for two of the college's star players. Now we're spending every day together as I try and save their grades, and I don't know if I'm crazy but it's like they both *want* me. I've never had a boyfriend. I'm not even out to my overbearing parents. How could I choose between them…or do I actually have to when they *both* want to be my Daddies? After my life comes crashing down, it's their turn to come to my rescue. Maybe what me and these god-like men have isn't just a fling after all?

*Heaven Sent is a steamy, standalone MMM romance. It's the first book in the **Paddle Creek College** series, where it's always the quiet ones who get up to the best kind of trouble. This book features a geek tutoring two hot jocks, two hot jocks tutoring a geek in a completely different way, a trash panda with a heart of gold, a human ice cream sundae, a revenge curse, and a guaranteed HEA with absolutely no cliffhanger.*

Click here to get the Heaven Sent eBook

PADDLE CREEK DADDIES #2: YES, SIR BY HJ WELCH

Two men. Two secrets. Can true love set them free?

BENEDICT

Just one more year, then I can go back to my beloved Oxford University and leave this tiny town behind me. Teaching is my passion, but I have other desires that I know would get me fired if anyone found out. The only trouble is, my new TA is pushing all my buttons and I'm not sure he even realizes what calling me Sir does to me. That's nothing, however, compared to when he starts calling me Daddy.

JACKSON

Have I got hots for teacher? Oh, yes. Messing around is off the table, though, so in a way it's safe to flirt with him and see him lose that stiff upper lip. It's not like he'd be interested in me anyway if he ever discovered what I love wearing under my clothes. Tough guys like me shouldn't like satin and lace. They shouldn't want to feel pretty. But Sir makes me feel gorgeous, and I want to be *such* a good boy for him.

*Yes, Sir is a steamy, standalone MM romance. It's the second book in the **Paddle Creek College** series, where it's always the quiet ones who get up to the best kind of trouble. This book features two people learning they don't have to be ashamed of who they are, a sassy brat who really wants to behave, a master in the bedroom who's a caring Daddy at heart, role playing so good it could win an Oscar, and a guaranteed HEA with absolutely no cliffhanger.*

Click here to get the Yes, Sir eBook

PADDLE CREEK DADDIES #3: LITTLE PLEASURES BY HJ WELCH

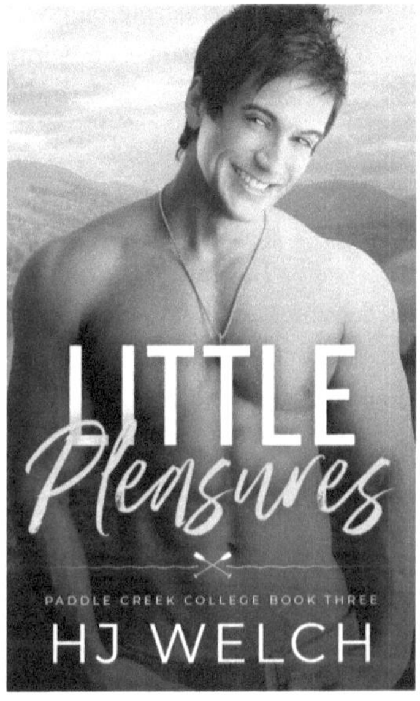

One jaded Daddy. One brand new boy. A fake relationship that becomes all too real.

XANDER

It's bad enough I have to move back to Paddle Creek with my awful stepmom, but now my half-brother's best friend has decided he has to look after me—even pretending to be my new boyfriend for a family wedding to keep my stepmother off my back. What Ruben doesn't know is that I've been in love with him for as long as I can remember and spending so much time with him is torture. Until it isn't. I can't believe that he's interested in me and even wants to be my Daddy, unlocking something in me I never knew was there. But when my stepmom goes too far, can I rely on Ruben to be there for me seeing as no one else in my life ever has?

RUBEN

When my life-long best friend asks me to keep an eye on his half-brother, of course I agree. Except he's a young man now, not a kid, and he's tugging at every single one of my Daddy heartstrings. Xander has just moved back into town and between finishing his degree, part-time work, and hellish stepmother, he's stressing himself into knots. It's a long time since a boy interested me, but I just want to protect Xander from the whole world. No matter the cost.

Little Pleasures is a steamy, standalone MM romance. It's the third book in the **Paddle Creek College** series, where it's always the quiet ones who get up to the best kind of trouble. This book features a Daddy introducing a boy to his inner little, the most loyal doggy best friend, a lot of dinosaurs, a heart-stopping rescue, and a guaranteed HEA with absolutely no cliffhanger. CW: Age play but no ABDL.

Click here to get the Little Pleasures eBook

PADDLE CREEK DADDIES #4: FOUR PLAY BY HJ WELCH

Three hungry wolves. One pretty little lamb. The hunt for love is on.

HARPER

I'm here for a good time, not a long time. When a total cutie asks me if I'd be interested in him and his two Daddies chasing me down and having their way with me, it sounds fun. I'm only in this crappy town for the summer, after all. But what we share is *intense.* I signed on to get caught…not to catch feels. However, when I find myself being hunted for real, can I really expect my wolf pack to come to the rescue?

RICK

After my husband and I swapped military life for married life, we quickly met our sweet baby boy who we'll do anything for. When Brady says he's found a sassy little lamb for the three of us to stalk, I'm happy to indulge him. But this broken young man swiftly captures all of our hearts, even though he says he can walk away any time. However, there's a difference between walking and being taken. Now I have the scent of a fool who's about to discover what happens when he's stolen what's *mine*.

Four Play is a super steamy, standalone MMMM romance. It's the fourth book in the **Paddle Creek College** series, where it's always the quiet ones who get up to the best kind of trouble. This book features exhilarating primal play, one hell of a paint ball match, an underwater themed motel, so many smooches, an obsessive ex-boyfriend, and a guaranteed HEA with absolutely no cliffhanger.

Click here to get the Four Play eBook

About the Author

HJ Welch is a British author of contemporary American MM small town series and books in multi authored shared universes, including the international number one best-selling Homecoming Hearts. She lives just outside of London with her husband and three balls of fluff that occasionally pretend to be cats.

She began writing at an early age, later honing her craft online in the world of fanfiction on sites like Wattpad. Fifteen years and over half a million words later, she sought out original MM novels to read. By the end of 2016 she had written her first book of her own, and in 2017 she achieved her lifelong dream of becoming a full-time author.

When she's not writing she's usually dancing, singing, filming music videos, taking long walks, working on jigsaw puzzles, drinking prosecco, or talking about Eurovision.

She also writes contemporary British MM fairy tale adaptation as Helen Juliet, including bestsellers Thorn in His Side, A Right Royal Affair, and Three.

———

You can contact Helen via the following:
Newsletter: https://www.subscribepage.com/helenjuliet
Website – www.hjwelch.com
Facebook Group – Helen's Jewels
Instagram – @helenjwrites

Twitter – @helenjwrites
Book Bub – @HJWelchAuthor
Facebook Page – @HJWelchAuthor